PRAISE FOR

CATHERINE McCARTHY

"With its complex characters and compelling mystery, *The House at the End of Lacelean Street* is a narrative joy to get lost in. McCarthy delivers the goods."

—Tim McGregor, author of *Eynhallow* and *Wasps in the Ice Cream*

"*Mosaic* is a great story, told by a deft writer. It's dark, it's brooding, and it'll have you on the edge of your seat."

—Ross Jeffery, Bram Stoker Award-nominated author of *The Devil's Pocketbook*

"Catherine's storytelling voice is something authoritative, assured. I'm a huge fan."

—Sadie Hartmann, Bram Stoker Award finalist and author of *101 Horror Books to Read Before You're Murdered*

"*Mosaic* is full of suspense and mysteries that whisper long after the story ends. I loved this book."

—Steph Nelson, author of *The Vein* and *The Final Scene*

THE
HOUSE
AT THE END OF
LACELEAN
STREET

CONTENT WARNING

This books is intended for mature audiences.

Reader discretion is advised.

Edited by Rob Carroll
Book Design and Layout by Rob Carroll
Cover Art by Tony Evans
Cover Design by Rob Carroll

ISBN 978-1-958598-23-8 (paperback)
ISBN 978-1-958598-68-9 (eBook)
darkmatter-ink.com

THE HOUSE AT THE END OF LACELEAN STREET

CATHERINE McCARTHY

To Tony...always.

CLAUDIA

CLAUDIA DANCE SITS on the aluminum bench, oblivious to the cold that seeps through her leggings and into her thighs. In the sleeve of her shirt is a paper tissue, sodden with tears and snot. She attempts to blow her nose, but the tissue's no longer fit for purpose. Claudia watches with disinterest as tiny paper particles float from her fingers onto the concrete, like miniature snowflakes.

Apart from the clothes on her back, the paper tissue is, or rather was, her only item of luggage. She does not consider the fact, nor does she know why she is sitting in a stone-cold bus shelter at midnight.

The amber glow from the street light opposite casts a spectral halo around her form, placing her in the spotlight. A gasp of air from the bus's brake pipe encourages her to get to her feet. Diesel-scented breath taints her lips as the bi-fold door opens.

The bus driver leans forward and beckons her aboard. "Lacelean Street." His voice has a gravel edge, though monotone, like a stick drawn across a sheet of corrugated card. A beckon is the only gesture he offers. No smile or frown. His expression is a blank sheet of paper.

Claudia climbs aboard. She does not pause to pay her fare, nor does it cross her mind to do so.

The driver does not wait for her to choose a seat. Instead, he pulls off without indicating or checking his mirrors.

Claudia moves down the aisle, grabbing the seat backs to steady herself, and chooses a window seat, halfway down on the left-hand side.

She is the only passenger on board.

The vibration from the wheels rumbles through her empty stomach, causing it to lurch left and right as the bus turns around corners. A faint smell of smoke hangs in the air. Smoke and stale sweat. Outside, a blanket of cloud soaks the streets in drizzle. It mists the windows so that everything and everyone is blurred.

Claudia leans back and closes her eyes.

"LACELEAN STREET." THE driver's voice startles her awake. Her mind is a stupor, filled with cotton wool that smells of bleach. Claudia wipes the windowpane with her sleeve, clearing an arc of condensation. Rainbow shaped, but colorless. No buildings in sight. Instead, the bus has stopped in front of tall metal gates, like those belonging to a mansion or park.

An elderly man with long gray hair and a tatty old coat clambers aboard. He limps down the aisle, his eyes fixed and weathered, and settles for a seat two rows in front of hers on the right. With a jolt and a hiss, the bus moves off, and the smell of smoke and sweat is joined by a whiff of wet dog that curdles her stomach.

Claudia stretches and yawns loudly, causing the driver to frown at her in his mirror. Not the man in the tatty coat, though. He doesn't even turn around. His head lolls to the side, and soon the rumble of wheels is accompanied by the rhythm of his snores. Claudia presses her forehead to the glass, relishing the cold damp against her skin. Cool. Soothing. Every bit of her hurts. Inside and out.

The lights of the city are a distant memory. It's so dark, Claudia can no longer see out. Even the night sky is hidden from view. And the drizzle has turned to rain that streaks down the windows in a gush of tears.

DAWN HAS ELBOWED a gap in night's shroud by the time the bus stops next. Claudia opens her eyes and sees it is no longer raining.

"Lacelean Street." The same two words, delivered in the same flat tone. The bus has stopped in the middle of nowhere. A barren wasteland of coarse grass and a road that's more dirt than Tarmac. A young woman boards, dressed head-to-toe in black. No more than a girl, really. Early twenties at most, pale complexion, pin-prick pupils, and earphones buried deep in her ears, from which the rhythmic rap of a male vocalist escapes. Claudia catches a waft of skunk and cheap lager as the woman passes by without so much as a glance and heads straight to the back of the bus.

SOME TIME LATER, as the sky daubs the world with bruises, the bus stops again. The driver glances in the rear-view mirror and repeats the only two words he knows. "Lacelean Street."

The girl is first to alight, even though she has the farthest to walk. Or stagger. The same song plays in her earphones, or at least Claudia thinks it's the same song. The girl pays Claudia and the man with the tatty coat no heed as she lurches down the aisle, fists clenched and nodding to the music. A wink of metal from her nose stud catches Claudia's eye. *Get up*, it says, and Claudia obeys. Her back is sore, her feet numb, so she propels herself down the aisle by using the seat backs as crutches. She dismounts the last step and takes a breath of stagnant air. Heavy. Laden with the previous night's rain.

She stands stock still, unsure of what to do next. It surprises her to see that the bus is bright yellow. Like butter. The color of a school bus.

The girl has crossed the road and sits cross-legged on the pavement opposite, rolling a joint. Her tongue darts snake-like as she licks the paper, and the fingers on her left hand clench and unclench in anticipation.

The man in the tatty coat struggles with the bottom step, which is too deep for his footing, and plummets head first onto the brittle grass at the side of the road. He lies there for a few seconds, unmoving, but it does not cross Claudia's mind to help him. Instead, she shields her eyes and squints in the direction of the sign across the road.

LACELEAN ST.

As the bus trundles off into the distance, Claudia watches it grow smaller and smaller until she can no longer distinguish the yellow from the gray.

The man is up on his feet, bent at the waist. Filthy hands press against his knees as he coughs and splutters, exhuming a gobbet of green phlegm onto the grass. Claudia turns her face away.

She looks left, then right, before crossing the road. Not because of the traffic, because there is none, but out of curiosity. Lacelean Street is nondescript. A long road of nothingness, with a single street sign. Wide pavements are lined with what she thinks are elm trees, the roots of which have pushed through the paving, turning the walkway into a deathtrap. Other than the trees, there is no visual clue to help her determine what to do next. No sounds to assist her. Nothing except a red-brick building at the furthest end of the road.

Ignoring her fellow passengers, she heads in that direction.

HOWARD

AS HOWARD WILSON sprawls face down in the dirt, he feels no embarrassment. His one concern is that Gus, his loyal friend of thirteen years, will be distressed. He closes his eyes and hears the whine of alarm, feels Gus's cold, wet snout pressed against his cheek, smells the warm pant of his breath.

"It's all right, boy. I'm not hurt." The vision of Gus motivates him to stand, a stabbing pain in his right shoulder makes him wince. He supports the injured arm at the elbow, before a hacking cough bends him double.

The world spins, blurs, and he wobbles. He does not trust his legs, nor does he trust his eyes right now because they seem to suggest that dawn has broken, and that cannot be the case. He gazes toward the sky, blinking at the cold wash of color, then his face crumples. Fat tears roll unchecked. They combine with the stream of snot to form a tributary above his lip. He sticks out his tongue and tastes the salty tang, then wipes his nose in his coat sleeve, grimacing with pain as he moves his arm.

Howard would like to sit and rest, but can see nowhere to do so. On the other side of the road, a young woman dressed in black has found somewhere to sit, but it's different for her. She can still cross her legs. If he were to sit cross-legged on the edge of the pavement, he might not get up again—not without both arms to propel him—and right now, he can't put weight on his shoulder.

"What shall we do now, Gus?" he murmurs, and waits for a reply. He nods his head, then shuffles to the other side of the road, still nursing the injured shoulder. In the distance he spies an older woman heading toward a red-brick building, so he follows in her footsteps.

As she enters the gate, he loses sight of her. His pace is slower, and he has to watch out for the cracks in the pavement. It's his age, and his shoulder , though he reckons she's no spring chicken either. He has to consider Gus, too, because Gus is still shaken from Howard's fall. He can tell by the way he whines and looks at Howard with huge brown eyes that would melt the coldest of hearts.

The woman has closed the metal gate behind her, leaving him to fumble with both lead and bolt with his left hand. Eventually he manages it, and the gate squeals open. It springs back as he passes through as if it's reluctant to let him out again. Ahead stands a tall Victorian building. It reminds him of a place he once knew, though he can't quite remember from where or when. "I hope they allow dogs," he says, glancing down. In his left hand he holds an invisible leash, the weight of his right arm now supported by the pocket of his coat. Each step he takes jars the shoulder joint, making his face contort with pain.

He is breathless and sweating despite the cold. It's the shock of the fall. He'll be fine once he's rested. Loose gravel crunches beneath his feet as he limps up the drive toward the house…or building, he's not sure which. It has a tall turret at the rear end, a bit like a German castle. Halfway up the drive, Howard pauses. He closes his eyes and tries to picture the gated entrance again. Had there been some kind of sign? If so, he'd missed it. No sign on the front of the building either, as far as he can see. Perhaps it's the woman's house. A moment of lucidity makes him wonder what the hell he's doing here.

His breath comes fast as he retraces his steps in his mind. He'd got off the bus. No, he'd fallen off the bus. He'd crossed the road and followed the woman, since there had been nowhere else to go. Ah, well, he's here now. With a little tug on the leash, he continues up the drive toward the front door.

STACEY

THE SPLIFF FAILS to hit the spot, no matter how hard Stacey drags on it. No matter how much she tries to hold the chemicals in her lungs. Her mobile phone shows NO SERVICE. Not a single fucking bar. Cheap piece of shit. Come to think of it, who does she want to call? She tucks the phone into her jacket pocket and rolls another joint.

The old guy across the road has face-planted in the dirt. She grins as he struggles to his feet, muttering incomprehensible words. Was he on the bus? Can't remember. He might have been. And what about the woman? Was she on the bus?

Stacey glances left and right, reaffirming the nothingness. Why the fuck did she get off the bus here? What had the driver called this place? She scratches her head, picks at a scab on her scalp, and examines it—wonders if scabs contain bacteria and whether it would be possible for someone to catch a disease from one—from her. If she had a disease, that is. Flicking the scab to the pavement, she turns to read the street sign behind her.

LACELEAN ST.

At least, she thinks that's what it says, but a few of the letters are hidden beneath a layer of grime. She spits on her palm and rubs at the dirt.

LACELEAN ST.

What kind of name is that? She's almost certain those were the words the bus driver had spoken, too.

The old man's up on his feet now, bent double and spewing something onto the grass. It might be vomit, or it might be phlegm. She can't tell from here.

The woman crosses the road and heads down the street. Stacey peers into the distance and spies a red-brick building. The woman's house, perhaps. Whatever.

Soon, the man follows in her footsteps, limping along and talking to himself, his left hand held at an angle as if dragging something. Except it isn't. Wacko! And people think she's weird!

She lies on the pavement, watching the sky morph lilac to slate, and smokes the second spliff. It'll rain soon. She can tell by the clouds.

Stacey Alloway, nineteen years old. She studies the brooding mass of sky, as well as the dark mass inside her head, in an effort to determine more about her life, but the information is missing. Blurred. Like an oil painting that's been rubbed while wet. She frowns at what's left of the spliff as if it is to blame, then pinches the tip between finger and thumb and throws it like a dart into the road.

She sits up and tunes in to the sound of the gutter that butts the pavement on her right. Iron grid and a dark hole. The water's too far down for her to see, but judging by the force of the gurgle, it rained heavily last night. She squeezes her eyes tight and tries to remember.

She'd been walking and walking for ages. Out beyond town and the suburbs. Wasteland. Scrub grass. Then the bus had pulled up, and she'd got on. And that's it. There's no more information buried in her gray matter. Fuck, that last spliff must have been strong.

She rummages about in her jacket and pulls out a tin and a lighter. Shoves a hand in the pocket of her jeans and pulls out a polythene bag containing white powder, though she has no recollection of having scored it. She pulls the seal and dips in a finger. Sniffs, then tastes it. Smack. No doubt about it. Bitter, with an undercurrent of cat piss. Good stuff, too. Almost pure white. Stacey removes a paper from the tin, rolls it, drizzles a line of powder on the lid and snorts. She lies back down on the pavement, face to the heavens, and enjoys the rush.

CLAUDIA

THE BLACK DOOR is high-gloss and much taller than an ordinary door, but then so is the house. Or building. Claudia's not sure which. It must be a house, otherwise there would be a sign. So what is she doing here? Her stomach flips, but her right hand reaches for the bell all the same. After three rings she considers giving up, but since she has nowhere else to go and nothing else to do, she persists. Still no one answers, even though the hall is lamplit.

Claudia takes three steps down from the porch and studies the house. The front door stands at an angle, on the corner of the building. At the farthest end there's a tower, like in a fairytale castle.

She follows the gravel path around to the left, shielding her eyes from the early-morning rays. It'll rain soon. Brooding clouds say so. The stone-mullion windows emit a warm glow from within, which suggests the house is occupied, but the windows are too high to see inside. Unless she retreats further and stands on the grass. She doesn't want to, though. Her shoes will get muddy. Claudia glances down at her feet, alarmed to discover

she is not wearing shoes at all. Instead, she is wearing
house-slippers. Fur-trimmed and grubby, with a hole in
the toe of the right one, through which a nail in desperate
need of a pedicure pokes. A moment of embarrassment,
and the misdemeanor is forgotten.

Claudia returns to the front door, grabs the brass handle,
and turns. It opens with a high-pitched yawn. High-ceilinged
hallway, black-and-white checkered tiles polished to a shine.
She steps into its warm arms, certain it has been waiting for
her. She stands stock-still and allows her weary eyes to take
in her surroundings. Deep skirtings, elaborate moldings,
and a small, round pedestal table upon which sits a folded
piece of card. Claudia picks it up and reads: *Claudia Dance.*

To the right of the table is a green velvet chair that looks
as if it belongs in the lounge of a high-class restaurant.
Not that she's ever been inside such an establishment, but
she's seen pictures in magazines. She perches on the edge
of the seat and opens the card.

Dear Claudia,

Welcome to the house on Lacelean St.

*Room One is located on the first floor, second door
on the right. Your key can be found in the drawer.*

May your stay here prove worthwhile.

Claudia's breath catches in her throat and stalls.
Room? Key? How do they know her name? Whoever
they are. She reads the note again in case her eyes are
deceiving her… *Your key can be found in the drawer.*
What drawer? She casts her gaze around the hall. A
walnut display cabinet, richly grained, with glass doors.

No drawer, though. She gets to her feet and wanders over. Three shelves, the top one displaying a variety of taxidermy—a gray squirrel clinging to a branch, and a pine marten bearing sharp teeth. The middle shelf is filled with minerals and ammonites in a variety of colors and sizes. The lower shelf is filled with miniature hats. Doll-sized, with hat-pins to match.

She faces the small table again. Only then does she see the drawer built into the apron. A miniature handle that she pinches between thumb and forefinger and pulls. Inside is a brass key to which a card label has been attached. It reads: *Room One, Claudia Dance*. She picks up both the key and card and sweeps up the stairs.

HOWARD

AS HOWARD APPROACHES the house, the first thing he notices is a dog bowl full of water at the bottom of the steps. "Here, Gus. You must be thirsty, boy." He wraps the imaginary leash around his left wrist and waits for Gus to quench his thirst. "Good boy, good boy," he mutters, glancing toward the front door.

It stands ajar, so Howard leans in and shouts hello. Nothing. He rings the bell and waits. Still nothing. Howard steps into the hall and drinks in the grand features. A grandfather clock strikes the hour. Eight o' clock, his usual breakfast time, and Gus's too. "I guess we'll have to wait, boy," he says. "I don't know about you, but this pain's stolen my appetite." The pain in his shoulder is a throbbing snake bite. The slightest move makes him wince.

He pats the pocket of his overcoat, hoping to discover a painkiller or two, but all he finds is an unwrapped mint toffee, complete with dog hair. He picks off the single strand and lays it in the palm of his hand as if it is the most precious gift in the world. And it is. It is!

Overcome, he slumps down on the velvet chair and sobs. He has forgotten the pain in his shoulder. Forgotten he is holding a dog's leash. This one hair, right here, contains the DNA of his beloved pet. If only they could use it to clone him, bring the dog back after it dies. He's read about stuff like that, seen it on TV, but he knows such a miracle of science is not yet possible. He holds the golden strand toward the chandelier, twirls it between finger and thumb while drying his eyes with the back of his good hand. The strand twinkles gold in the light, sparking an idea. He will keep the hair in case someone develops the technology to clone Gus even after the dog is gone. It's not impossible. Not at all. Nothing's impossible. He rummages in the pocket of his trousers and pulls out a soiled handkerchief, then wraps the single hair and cossets it back in the pocket.

On the little side-table next to where he sits is a card. It has been folded in half, like a place-marker at a wedding or an elaborate dinner. On the front, in gold lettering, is his name: *Howard Wilson.* He opens the flap and reads.

> *Dear Howard,*
>
> *Welcome to the house on Lacelean St.*
>
> *Room Two is located on the first floor at the far end of the landing. Your key can be found in the drawer.*
>
> *May your stay here prove worthwhile.*

He slides open the drawer, picks up the key, and leans down to ruffle Gus's fur. "Come on, boy. We have a room waiting for us."

As he climbs the stairs, Howard concludes that the house is in fact a hotel. A hotel that welcomes dogs, all too rare these days. Strange, because there's no guestbook to sign or reception desk to check-in at. No name on the gates or front of the house to assist its guests in finding it. He can't remember making a reservation, but he might have. His head's been in such a muddle lately, it's hard to think straight. Never mind, he's made it this far. "Things can only get better, hey, Gus?" The dog's name tag clinks as they climb the stairs.

STACEY

DESPITE THE RAIN soaking her face, Stacey's skin
is flushed. The rush from the smack has subsided, and
now her mouth is dry as a desert, limbs heavy as lead. She
couldn't stand even if she wanted to. She doesn't, though.
She's more than happy to stay sprawled on the pavement,
face to the heavens, and allow the drizzle to cool her skin.
The Notorious B.I.G.'s *Suicidal Thoughts* plays in her ears,
matches her throbbing heart beat for beat, measured
against the Tarmac. The lyrics were written for her, she's
certain. Not right now, though, because right now she
feels *GOOD!* She'd switch tracks if she could be arsed,
but her fingers feel like they belong to the purple dude
from *Monsters, Inc.* All skinny, with bulbous tips. They'd
probably fail to cooperate. What was the character's name?
Randy Dog or something. She giggles. Laughs so hard
her stomach hurts. Then she curls into a ball and sleeps.

BY THE TIME Stacey reaches the brick building, the
sun has chased away the rain clouds and has warmed

the earth enough to persuade her to remove her leather jacket. It's slung over her shoulder, exposing the tattoo of a cobra hidden amongst roses that snakes its way from shoulder to elbow. A nickel chain around her neck is adorned with a skull charm. Its red-gemmed eyes are the only color she wears, apart from the tattoo.

When she reaches the brick building, she fails to notice the lack of signage on the gate. Her Dr. Martens have brought her here, and that's all that matters. Instead of ringing the bell, she grabs hold of the brass knocker and gives it three loud whacks. While she waits, she examines its intricate design, traces an index finger along the ridged ram's horns. Its eyes are closed, but she's certain it sees her. The thin *skin* covering its eyelids flickers. Just once. Cool! Then the door opens.

Standing, hands on hips, is a middle-aged woman dressed in a pale gray leisure suit. "You're late," the woman says, and Stacey scowls.

The woman opens the door wide and ushers her in. "We've been waiting for you to arrive, and now we've missed the first lesson." Stacey stifles a giggle and wonders what the fuck the woman is on about. Plus, the woman doesn't look as if she belongs in this house. Her leisure suit is coffee-stained and made of cheap fleece, the kind you can buy in any supermarket or discount store. Her hair is brassy; the middle parting shows an inch or more of dark roots, threaded with gray.

Without wiping her feet, Stacey steps inside and casts her gaze around the hall. "Woah! Do you live here?" She sniffs and wipes her nose on the back of her hand.

The woman opens her mouth to speak, then closes it again, as if she is uncertain how to answer. Instead, she strides across the hall. It's the walk that does it, a kind of swaying sashay that belies the rest of her appearance. Stacey's seen her before. "Were you on the bus?"

The woman stops in front of a door and turns to face her. Her expression is blank, dead eyes, as if the light has been extinguished. She nods, just once, then opens the door.

The smell of freshly roasted coffee hangs in the air. It battles a dirtier smell of wet dog and unwashed bodies. Stacey sees the culprit sitting on a parlor chair in front of the bay window. It's the old man from the bus. She's certain it's him, though he also wears a pale gray leisure suit, identical to the woman's. Despite the scent of wet dog, Stacey's stomach rumbles. She cannot remember the last time she ate.

The woman hears the rumble. "There are cookies on the tray, but the coffee is cold." She gestures toward a sideboard set with silverware and a bone china tea set. "If you'd arrived when you were supposed to, you could have had breakfast."

Stop nagging, for fuck's sake. Stacey barely manages to keep the words under wraps. What's all this about being late? And what did the woman mean when she said they'd missed the first lesson? She picks up a chocolate digestive and crams it in her mouth. It tastes good, though the chocolate has melted a little in the overly heated room. She pours a cup of lukewarm coffee, picks up a second cookie, flops down on a sofa, and throws several cushions to the floor before putting her feet up. No one chastises her. In fact, neither of them seem to notice. The man is talking to himself again, watery eyes fixed on the view outside the window. The woman has moved to the far end of the grand room, where she stands in front of a blazing fireplace, wringing her hands.

Stacey downs her coffee in two gulps and sits up.

"Your card is in the hall, on the round table," the woman says. "Your key is probably in the drawer." And with that, she glides from the room, closing the door behind her.

The old man continues to stare out of the window, lost in his own world.

Stacey gets to her feet, yawns and stretches, then returns to the hall. On the round table is a small folded card. She picks it up and reads her name, written in elaborate gold lettering: *Stacey Alloway.* She sniffs, then clears her throat with a loud hack that produces a loogie. Not knowing what to do with the phlegm, she opens the front door, aims, and spits at a stone gargoyle. She cheers when it lands on her target's heavy brow. The gargoyle turns its head and glares at her, nostrils flared and claws bared.

Back in the hall, she picks up the card again and reads.

Dear Stacey,

Welcome to the house on Lacelean St.

Room Three is located on the second floor at the far end of the landing. Your key can be found in the drawer.

May your stay here prove worthwhile.

CLAUDIA

BACK IN HER room, Claudia removes the sweatshirt and slings it on the bed before entering the bathroom. They're still there, the bruises. In the mirror above the basin she examines the purple ring around her neckline, prodding thumb-shaped marks until she can no longer stand the pain. She'd scrubbed so hard in the shower earlier. Surely they should have faded. Deep in the pit of her belly, a breathy voice whispers—a man's voice—vaguely familiar. *You can't wash away the brand of punishment. Time and good behavior are the only remedies. But don't worry, they'll be hidden beneath your clothing.* She fills the basin with hot water, swirls in a generous dollop of coconut shower gel, and proceeds to scrub at the marks with a washcloth until her neck is red and raw.

The marks around her wrists are less painful, but just as stubborn. She pats the skin dry and stares at herself in the mirror. Gaunt. Hollow eye sockets and sallow skin. Hooded lids and crow's feet that extend almost as far as the temple. Fifty-three, but she looks a decade older.

Claudia flattens her hair on either side of her parting and groans. When did she last color it? Can't remember. She plucks a few gray hairs and drops them into the basin, watches them float aimlessly on what's left of the foam. She pulls the plug and stares trance-like as the water swirls and disappears, startled by the final glug.

Returning to the bedroom, she pulls the sweatshirt over her head and arranges the neckline so that the bruises are hidden. Her own clothes, those she arrived in, had disappeared when she went down for breakfast, yet so far she's heard no one come and go. No sign of a maid or resident other than her and the old man. And now the girl has joined them, so tomorrow they will have their first lesson.

She picks up the black file marked *Rules* and skims the contents once more.

For the duration of your stay, you must remain within the boundary.

Lessons will take place in the library at 09:00 prompt. Tardiness will not be tolerated!

A stab of chest pain accompanies the reading of Rule Two. Both she and the old man had found their way to the library by 08:50, but the door remained firmly locked till well past 09:00. It was the girl's fault. They weren't allowed in without all three of them present. She reads the last sentence again: *Tardiness will not be tolerated!* What punishment might be meted out as a result of them missing the first lesson? And all because the girl arrived late. It isn't fair. Her eyes sting with tears, and her hand strokes the skin on her neck. Maybe they won't be, but not knowing is worse.

Please treat the house with respect.

This rule also worries her because of the girl. She noticed the way she'd sprawled on the sofa without removing her boots. She'd said nothing at the time, but only because the girl had just arrived and hadn't had a chance to read the rules.

DO NOT CLIMB THE STAIRS IN THE LIBRARY UNTIL YOU HAVE BEEN GIVEN PERMISSION TO DO SO.

This last rule worries her least, despite it being written in capital letters. Whoever wrote it might well be implying it's the most important rule, but she has no intention of climbing any tower. She's acrophobic—afraid of heights.

Claudia lies on the bed and considers the strangeness of the situation. Why is she here? And why can't she remember the past? She closes her eyes and thinks hard, but apart from her name and age, she can recall very little. Is she married? Does she have children? A job? Why are her neck and wrists black and blue with bruises?

The pulse in her neck throbs with anxiety. Maybe she's dead. Perhaps this house is some kind of purgatory, a holding place where those recently deceased await judgment before being sent on. The old man looks as though he's on death's door, but what about the girl? She's young, yes, but far from healthy. Perhaps she, too, is dead. An overdose, or suicide.

But if they're dead, what's the point in having lessons in the library? Christ, at fifty-three, what can she possibly learn? Unless she's forgotten all that has come before and has to start from scratch. She tests herself mentally. *Two*

plus two equals four. The fourth letter of the alphabet is D.
How come she's able to recall facts like this but nothing
else? Nothing personal?

Something else strikes her as odd. How do the owners
of this place know coconut shower gel is her favorite? And
how do they know she eats muesli for breakfast? Maybe
it's a coincidence. Yet the old man had been given a plate
of bacon and eggs. No one brought it, yet there it was, all
hot and bothered beneath the silver domed lid. So why
was she given muesli?

She thinks again about breakfast. After her arrival,
there'd been time for a quick shower, then she'd changed
into the leisure suit that had been left on the bed, and
shortly after she'd gone downstairs.

Neither of them spoke while they ate. They didn't even
exchange names. A place had been set for him at one end
of the long table, and a place for her at the other end. No
place had been set for the girl. The man hadn't showered,
and he smelled of wet dog and stale body odor. She caught
whiffs of it while she ate. If he didn't shower soon, she'd
have to tell him.

Claudia picks up the file marked *Guest Information* and
opens it again to the page marked *Mealtimes.*

Breakfast 08:00

Lunch 12:30.

Dinner 07:30

She glances at the clock on the dressing-table. 12:15.
She isn't the least bit hungry, but she will do as she's told
and go down for lunch at the appropriate time so as not
to upset her host.

HOWARD

THE ALDER BUCKTHORN outside the bay window bears dark berries, which suggests autumn is on its way. Howard remembers that the buckthorn's charcoal is prized for its use in the manufacture of gunpowder, though he fails to recall which trees grow in his own garden. Right now, he cannot even picture his own garden. He considers the alder buckthorn an unusual specimen for such a formal space as this. Manicured lawn, mathematically precise flower beds, even the odd topiary here and there.

"Fancy a walk?" He smiles down at the space beside the chair and waits for Gus to whine. The tinkle of the dog's name tag lets him know the animal is eager, so he gets to his feet, straightens his spine, and shuffles toward the front door.

During breakfast, Howard was concerned that Gus hadn't eaten, so he had slipped him a rasher of bacon under the table. He will do the same during lunch, which he hopes will be roast beef and Yorkshire pudding. His stomach growls at the thought. He glances at his wrist and realizes he's not wearing his watch. Was he wearing it when he arrived?

The gray joggers and sweatshirt had been folded neatly on the bed. They'd smelled of lily of the valley, and felt soft against his stubble. He'd changed into them, leaving his old clothes in a heap on the carpet. There'd been slippers, too. Fur-lined but sturdy. Good enough to walk the grounds in. He wiggles his toes, enjoying the comfort. By now he has forgotten all about the watch because the image of his trousers in a heap on the carpet reminds him of something else. Something far more important. The single hair, wrapped in a handkerchief that he left in his trouser pocket. He would like to go back to his room and check that it's still there, but Gus is enjoying the fresh air. He'll need to put it somewhere safe when he returns to the room. He can't bear to lose it.

His shoulder gives a stab, reminding him that four hours have passed since he took the painkillers that had been left on the breakfast table beside the glass of orange juice. He hopes another two pills will appear at lunch.

Howard spots a garden bench at the far end of the lawn and heads in that direction. Once seated, he releases the catch on Gus's leash and allows the dog to run free, smiling at the pant of his breath and the pounding of his paws on the grass. He closes his eyes. Apart from the high-pitched ringing of his tinnitus, he hears nothing. No birdsong, no traffic, not a sound from inside the house. There's a faint rustle of leaves, and that's it.

He looks back at the house. The dining room is lamplit, as is one of the bedrooms on the first floor, which he assumes must be the woman's—the older woman's, not the younger. The younger woman must either be sitting in the dark, or her room is at the back of the house.

He knows it's almost time for lunch because he remembers the grandfather clock chiming midday as he left the hall. The file in his room states lunch at twelve-thirty, therefore they (whoever *they* are) must be in the dining room right now, laying up. Howard is mildly curious as to who *they* might be, but as long as he and Gus are fed and watered, he doesn't really care.

He gives a whistle and waits for Gus to come running. He hooks the dog to the leash and heads inside, eager to check on the handkerchief in his trouser pocket.

The clock in the hall says twenty past twelve, so he hurries up the stairs. He does not want to be late for lunch because both he and Gus are famished.

To his dismay, his clothes have disappeared. A groan of despair escapes his lips and panic ensues. He flings open the wardrobe door, disappointed to find it empty. Even his coat and shoes are missing. He checks all the drawers and the bathroom, but finds nothing. Assuming a maid has taken his clothes to launder, he hurries downstairs, tripping over the rug in the hall in his haste, and jarring his bad shoulder.

Red-faced and breathless, he rushes into the dining room, expecting to find a maid setting the table.

"Hello?" he calls, but his desperate cry is met with silence. He dashes from the room, bumping into Claudia on her way in. He does not apologize, because there is only one thing on his mind. He must be reunited with the dog's hair.

Sobbing, he yanks at one door handle after another, desperate to find someone, *anyone,* who might be able to tell him the whereabouts of his clothes. Each and every room is either locked or empty. His panic echoes around the hall, causing Claudia to hesitate before tasting her vegetable soup. She stops, spoon poised mid-air, as Howard reappears.

"I can't find anyone! They've stolen my trousers." His nose drips tears onto the starched white tablecloth, and he tugs at the front of his sweatshirt like a toddler mid-tantrum.

Claudia looks away. She tastes the soup, which is perfectly seasoned, and ignores him.

Howard leans on the table in front of his place setting and continues to sob. A heaving, uncontrollable mess that makes the smell of warm dog more potent, so much so that Claudia is forced to put down her spoon.

She is about to speak when the door bursts open and in walks the girl, still dressed in black. Ignoring both her and the man, she scans the table until she locates her place setting, then she lifts the silver lid covering the plate and gasps. "Pepperoni pizza! My favorite." Without taking a seat, she picks up a slice and shovels it in her mouth, letting the cheese dangle as she tilts her head back.

Howard continues to wail. The pain in his shoulder has returned. Nursing the limb with his good arm, he rocks on his heels.

Stacey drags out a chair, the noise temporarily drowning out the wails. She is halfway through the second slice of pizza when Claudia interrupts. "What on earth is the matter?" Her soup spoon clatters against the side plate as she glares at him.

"My trousers. They've taken my trousers!" He continues to wail, louder now that he has her attention.

Claudia wrinkles her nose in distaste. "Well, they probably need to be washed." She points at his joggers. "You have those, so stop fussing."

"But—" Howard is about to say more, but changes his mind and slumps down on the chair in defeat.

Stacey follows the discussion as though watching a tennis match, an amused smirk on her face. She lets rip an enormous burp. "Ah," she says. "That's better."

Claudia tuts, then picks up her spoon and returns to her soup, while Howard removes the lid from his plate and pouts at his roast beef and Yorkshire pudding. Gradually, the sobs lessen and become a shudder.

Claudia wipes the corners of her mouth in her napkin and stands. As she does so, Howard picks up a slice of beef, dripping in gravy, and throws it on the floor.

"Rules!" Claudia shouts, slamming the heels of her hands on the table. "Didn't you read the file? Treat this house with respect!"

Howard's bottom lip quivers, but he looks beyond her as though she is invisible, and turns his attention to the garden.

Claudia storms from the room.

Stacey bundles the remaining slices of pizza into her napkin and follows close behind.

He is all alone again. Almost. "Good boy," he says, leaning sideways. "Was the beef tasty?"

STACEY

THE GRAY LEISURE suit remains folded on the bed. No way is she wearing that piece of shit. She'd rather die. Her room is immaculate but depressing. The comforter is far too chintzy, like something an old woman would choose—the matching curtains, too.

Stacey opens the window and looks down on a courtyard and what appears to be a stable block. Would the owners let her ride? If they keep horses, that is. Just because the house has a stable block doesn't mean there are horses. She pokes her nose out of the window and inhales, but all she can smell is pizza and nicotine, which reminds her, it's been more than an hour since she had a smoke. She pats the pocket of her jacket and pulls out her stash. Shit, there's enough to last till tomorrow, but then it'll be gone. Panic swells in her throat, threatening to choke her.

She whips out her mobile and scrolls the list of contacts, stopping at *Reeta*. She fails to summon an image of Reeta to mind, and yet she senses a connection to the name. A drug connection. Only then does she notice the words NO SERVICE. Not a single freaking bar! Same thing had happened when she sat on the pavement. It's like this place is in a tunnel or under a mountain or something. How is she supposed to arrange a deal when she can't call anyone? It's unlikely the old man or the woman will be carrying anything, though both appear to be on something, judging by their behavior. Fucking nuts, the pair of them.

No sign of a phone in the room, so she grabs the *Guest Information* file and flicks through, desperate to find something about mobile connectivity, a landline, or even Broadband. Anything will do.

She is sorely disappointed.

She pockets the mobile and stomps from the room, leaving the grease from the napkin-wrapped pizza to seep onto the comforter.

Stacey hasn't read the file marked *Rules*, nor does she intend to, therefore she has no idea that Rule One states she should remain within the boundary.

She wanders the garden, phone in hand, waving it about in a desperate attempt to get a signal. When this fails, she jogs down to the gate and yanks the handle, but the gate is locked. In the few hours she has been here, someone has fitted a sturdy chain around the posts, as well as a padlock fit for a prison. Fuck! To make matters worse, the gate is attached to a perimeter fence that is eight feet tall by her estimate, and slippery as an eel. She steps back and gazes upwards at the pointed tips. How the fuck is she supposed to get out of here? Her mouth fills with sand, blood pounds in her ears, and her arms and legs go limp.

She kicks at the loose gravel, cursing the place to hell and back, then walks the perimeter just to be certain. Her instinct is correct, the fence runs the entire length, but there does seem to be a potential weak spot in the fortifications, where a tall tree grows close to the fence at the farthest corner. If she could find a way to climb the tree, she might be able to scale the fence. But the lowest branch is way above her reach. She'd need a ladder, or a foot-up at least. If she can't find a ladder, she'll ask the old man to give her a foot-up, though she's not sure he's strong enough to take her weight. She thinks back to the dining room where he stood blubbering and nursing his right arm. Shit. In that case, it'll have to be the woman. Stacey will bully her into helping, if need be.

Squatting beside a rose bush, she takes out her tin and rolls a smoke. The little bag of white powder is close to empty. It stares back at her, pale-faced and forlorn. Stacey knows it contains enough for one decent line and that's it. Will she be able to resist using it tonight? Probably not, judging by the way her nerves are feeling. She's all hyper, like a jackal caught in a trap.

The floral scent from the roses mingles with the spicy scent of skunk, making her lightheaded. Overcome with a sense of nostalgia, she plucks a rose from a stem and puts it to her nose. Tears prick her eyes. She hasn't cried in years. Many, many years. At least she doesn't think she has. Why now? Is it because she feels trapped? Backed into a corner like some feral alley cat?

She bends the stem of the rose so that the sharpest thorn pokes outwards, then digs the thorn deep into the tender skin beneath her fingernails, splicing left to right until blood trickles down the chipped black varnish. By the time she's finished, her fingers run red. The pain offers little relief. It is insufficient to quell the ferocious beast that has awoken within her.

CLAUDIA

THERE'S NO TV in her room, no telephone either, but Claudia doesn't mind. She takes a long nap before wandering the garden. The floral borders are well kept, though she can't name any of the flowers. Their colors remain vibrant despite the chill in the air that suggests it's late summer or early autumn. She's not sure which.

Several trees are dotted here and there, some with leaves tinted red and gold, and some that bear fruit—apples, and something that looks like an apple crossed with a pear. Somewhere deep in her brain lurk the words to an old rhyme:

> *They dined on mince and slices of quince,*
> *which they ate with a runcible spoon.*

Quince. She's sure it's the name of the fruit on this tree. But what's a runcible spoon? She must remember to ask the teacher when she attends tomorrow's lesson. *There you go, Claudia. That's something you can still learn at the age of fifty-three.* She smiles at the thought, but the smile is replaced with a worried frown when she thinks about the girl. What if she doesn't get up in time for the lesson? Surely they'll be punished if they miss a second one.

Claudia glances left and right in case anyone is watching, then tugs a quince from the tree and wanders over to a bench that hides beneath the shade of a much taller tree. She wipes the quince on the sleeve of her fleece and takes a bite. Woody flesh, sour taste. She spits it out just in time to see a maggot wriggle from the seedy core.

Thief, a voice in her head chides, and Claudia throws the fruit onto the lawn and swallows the bile that rises to her throat.

The wind gusts a swirling breath, sending a flurry of sycamore seeds onto her lap. She shivers, picks one up and examines it. Twin blades, shaped like a helicopter or the wishbone of a chicken carcass. She thinks about making a wish, but doesn't know what to wish for, so she flicks the seed into the wind and watches it spiral through the air before landing on the ground. With a bit of luck, the pod will germinate in the shade of its parent and become a new tree. A predator might get to it first, though. A fox, or a squirrel, perhaps, or a bird. The likelihood of that little seed maturing is tiny. Its prospects for survival are bleak.

CLAUDIA IS NOT surprised when the girl doesn't show at dinner. She sits at the opposite end of the table to the old man and picks at her shepherd's pie. It's one of her favorites, but she can't get the image of the maggot out of her head. Each mouthful she takes is preceded by a thorough examination of what's on the fork, in case a maggot or some other grub is lurking.

After four or five mouthfuls, she gives up and pushes the plate away. The atmosphere in the room is discomforting. Somewhere deep inside her, there exists a pocket of sympathy for the man, but she seems unable to locate it. Far more palpable is a sense of emptiness.

She studies his face as he fusses over a plate of fish and chips, picking out skinny bones with greasy fingers and peeling back gray skin before forking out the white flesh. He has a fair appetite for a man his age. She wishes he wouldn't throw scraps on the floor, though. The floor's solid wood—*parquet,* she thinks it's called. A geometric pattern, polished to a shine. Easy to clean, no doubt, but it's disrespectful all the same. She wants to reprimand him but feels less feisty than during lunch. She'll let it slide this time, but if it happens again, she'll have a word.

When at last the plate is nothing but a heap of skin and bone, he puts it to one side and turns his attention to dessert. Rice pudding—the homemade kind—thick and creamy, with a skin speckled with nutmeg. He rubs his hands together and tucks in, while she eyes her poached pear in red wine with contempt. Why is each of them given something different? She thinks back to the three meals she's had so far, all of which have consisted of her favorite foods. Apart from the pear in wine. She wonders if someone was watching her out in the garden. Perhaps they saw her steal a quince from the tree. Maybe they knew about the maggot, too.

Maybe they even planted it there.

You cannot *plant* a maggot in a fruit, she tries to reason with herself. But you can't board a bus at midnight, either. Not without intention. You can't travel through the night and find yourself in the only building on an unfamiliar street, far from home, with two strangers, one of whom stinks of wet dog and throws food on the floor, and the other who has no manners whatsoever and is likely to bend and break every rule in the book—if she even reads the book, that is.

Filled with despair, Claudia pushes her chair back and heads up to bed.

THE NEXT MORNING it's just her and the old man at breakfast. Another no-show for the girl, which also suggests she's unlikely to appear for their lesson. Claudia's skin prickles, beads of sweat dampen her scalp. She eyes the clock on the wall, counting each swing of the pendulum as it ticks away the seconds.

Her cornflakes turn to mush in the bowl. A skin forms on the top of her cup of tea. She has no appetite this morning. A flick of the old man's wrist suggests he's thrown something on the floor. A kipper, no doubt. The smoked fish stinks, and her stomach turns. She stares at him through narrowed eyes, but his own are focused on the food on his plate: bread and butter, cut in triangles; a second kipper, slathered in butter. If he enjoys it so much, why on earth is he throwing it on the floor?

The clock chimes the half hour, which means it won't be long before their lesson is due. She hasn't been in the library yet. She knows where it is. Ground floor, fourth door on the left, labeled with a brass plaque—*Library.*

Claudia pushes back the chair and stands, addressing the old man who is busy wiping up kipper grease with the last remaining bread-and-butter triangle. "Don't forget, lesson at nine."

He does not appear to hear, or if he does, he chooses to ignore the comment, and Claudia feels herself bristle.

Back in her room, she brushes her hair and cleans her teeth, wishing she could add a touch of lipstick to brighten her sallow complexion. Whoever runs this place has provided the basics but no frivolities.

What will the teacher be like? What kind of lessons will they receive? She smooths imaginary creases out of her sweatshirt and heads downstairs.

Ten minutes to nine, according to the grandfather clock in the hall. Neither the old man nor the girl have arrived yet. She opens the front door and takes a few deep breaths in an attempt to quell the ferocious heat that has risen to her cheeks. The back of her neck is sweaty; damp hair clings to her forehead. Hormonal flush or anxiety? She's not sure which. Both, perhaps.

A moment of relief when she hears the old man's footsteps on the stairs—a shuffling, padding sound that lacks enthusiasm.

She and the man wait at the door marked *Library* like a pair of silent statues. Every few seconds, she glances at the clock, hoping the girl will appear. At five to nine, she turns to the man with a look of fierce determination. "Right, let's go get her."

He follows her up the stairs like a lamb.

Claudia isn't sure which room has been assigned to the girl, but thinks it's on the second floor. The old man lags several stairs behind and is breathless by the time they reach the first-floor landing. She does not wait for him to catch up. Instead, she continues to climb until she reaches the second floor, then proceeds to knock on each and every door, rattling their handles until she finds one unlocked.

By the time she opens it, the old man has almost caught up.

Claudia pokes her head around the door and peers into the gloom. A humid stink and drawn curtains suggest the girl is still in bed. Claudia throws the door wide open and enters.

The girl lies on top of the bed in a fetal position, fully clothed. She snores lightly, a trickle of drool at the corner of her mouth. Claudia pulls back the curtains and daylight floods the room. Arms folded, she stands beside the bed, frowning. The alarm clock reads 08:58. Two minutes to countdown.

"Get up," she says, her tone firm and self-assured, but the girl does not stir. Claudia shakes her by the shoulder and repeats the command. No response, apart from a slight moan.

"Grab her arm. She's coming whether she likes it or not," she says to the man, and together they drag her off the bed, propping her up on either side. The girl's black-booted toes trail the landing as they drag her toward the first flight of stairs.

"The fuck?" she murmurs, as they bump against the hand rail.

"Hold tight," Claudia says. The old man attempts to steady himself against the banister.

Eventually, by luck rather than judgment, they reach the hall at the exact moment the clock strikes nine.

By now, the girl is semiconscious. She moans under her breath and elbows both her assailants, but is too drugged to protest harshly. Pinprick pupils, pasty complexion. Howard bears her weight while Claudia grabs the handle of the door marked *Library* and turns.

HOWARD

BY THE TIME they reach the hall, Howard is exhausted. Bent double, he swallows mouthful after mouthful of saliva, gasping for breath. The girl slumps against him, feet outstretched and head lolling. Her eyes are closed, but the lids twitch, as if a colony of tiny ants march beneath them.

"Well, what are you waiting for?" the woman says, and Howard remembers they have come for their first lesson. He hopes the subject is horticulture. But more importantly, he will finally get the chance to ask someone about his missing trousers. In all honesty, it is the only reason he agreed to help drag the girl out of bed.

Propping the girl against the wall, he follows the woman into the library, surprised to find no one there. It's a circular room, lined floor to ceiling with books in dark oak cases. The smell of old paper and a hint of camphor tickles his nose, making him sneeze. The library is in the tower then? His eyes water as he drinks in the atmosphere. A wrought-iron spiral staircase in the far corner leads to the upper floor, where darkness reigns. But this room on the ground floor is bright. Dust motes dance in front of the bay window overlooking the gardens. Sparkling specks of learning that have escaped the pages they were written on.

In front of the fireplace stand three wooden desks. Old-fashioned school desks, but adult-sized. Each has a sloping lid, an inkwell in the corner that bleeds a blue-black stain, and a wooden chair to match. Facing them is a larger version of the same desk—the teacher's desk—but no teacher sits behind it.

Together, they drag the girl into the library and sit her at the middle desk so it will be more difficult for her to escape, should she become capable of doing so. She rouses a little, then tucks her legs beneath the chair, folds her arms on the desk, and rests her head. Within seconds, she is fast asleep.

Howard takes the desk on her right, and the woman sits on her left, her mouth pinched with anticipation.

"Lie down," Howard whispers, pointing toward the floor.

Apart from their breath and the distant tick of a clock, the room is silent. Both he and the woman glance in the direction of the door from time to time, expecting the teacher to arrive at any moment. On the teacher's desk, Howard spies three old-fashioned sweet jars made of glass, each with stopper lid—the kind that makes a slurping sound when you open it, like a genie escaping from a bottle. Howard knows what he would wish for. He screws up his eyes and peers closer, wishing he'd remembered to bring his spectacles when he left home. Inside the jars are not sweets, but colored chalks, or at least he thinks that's what they are. It's difficult to tell from this distance. The front of each jar is labeled, though he cannot read what it says because the writing is too small.

Beside the fireplace stands a tall wooden chalkboard on wheels, complete with narrow shelf, over which a cloth is draped. Words are written on the board. Words in immaculate cursive handwriting, the kind of writing he hasn't seen in a long time. The message is difficult to read from where he sits, but he thinks it says something like: *Choose a chalk and hand it to the tea—*

He is still trying to decipher the writing when the woman pipes up, "Choose a chalk and hand it to the teacher. When the lesson has been learned, you may wipe the slate clean."

Howard fidgets in his seat. The pain in his shoulder has worsened because of having to drag the girl, and the small of his back is feeling its age against the upright chair. He wishes the teacher would arrive soon because he is desperate to ask about his trousers. He glances at the clock. Ten past nine. Didn't the rulebook state they should attend lessons promptly and that tardiness would not be tolerated? Well, it's a shame the teacher isn't obeying his own rules. Or her rules. It could be a woman, but Howard thinks it'll be a man. A strict, headmasterly type, complete with flowing black cloak, a cane, and pince-nez.

As he's considering this, the woman rises from her seat and approaches the teacher's desk. She picks up a jar and plonks it down on the desk in front of the girl. "Wake up!" she hisses, but the girl does not flinch.

She picks up another jar and places it in front of Howard, then takes the final jar and puts it on her own desk. Howard sees that the label bears his name—*Howard Wilson.* He is pleased to note that he guessed correctly about the jars being full of chalks, even though he'd rather them be full of Liquorice Allsorts. Liquorice Allsorts are his favorite, especially the black rolls with white icing. Gus doesn't like Liquorice Allsorts. He sniffs, whines his disapproval, then moves away when Howard eats them. The thought of a Liquorice Allsort makes Howard's mouth water. He runs his tongue around bare gums, imagining the sticky liquorice on his teeth. Except his teeth are not there. His stomach plummets as he realizes he has arrived minus his spectacles *and* his dentures. And he paid such a lot of money for them, too. No wonder he had trouble chewing his bacon.

He pulls at the glass stopper, rejoicing in the whoosh of air that escapes, and makes a silent wish. His hand is too big to fit inside, so he tilts the jar on its side and pulls out a pale-green chalk—the first to slip from the bundle. It sparks a memory. A memory of childhood, and a school-room not dissimilar to the space he's currently sitting in. He closes his eyes and allows the memory to take shape. *Howard Wilson*, a stern voice in his head says, *Can you not spell disenchantment? Shame on you!* A black cloak, a cane. His eyes spring open, and he gasps. The woman is watching him, her gaze wary.

"Give it to me," she says, holding out her hand, palm up.

He passes her the pale-green chalk, and she strides over to the blackboard. He imagines she will write the word *disenchantment*, spelling it out perfectly, letter by letter, perhaps, or by splitting the word into syllables. But she doesn't. Instead, she cleans the board with the cloth and proceeds to write something entirely different.

What she writes shakes him to his core:

> *Gus is dead. You buried him in the garden, beneath the dogwood tree, because the dogwood represents loyalty, and Gus was the most loyal friend you ever had.*

The message steals Howard's breath. A mournful wail rises from breastbone to lips, causing the woman to cover her ears as it escapes.

He gets to his feet and staggers from the room, leaving behind the smell of wet dog and body odor.

Howard makes his way to the farthest corner of the garden and slumps on a bench beneath the sycamore tree. The tips of its leaves shine gold. The mid-morning sun peeks through its splayed fingers and warms his gray complexion.

His fists are clenched, his bowels knotted. Imprinted indelibly in his mind are the words, *Gus is dead. You buried him in the garden, beneath the dogwood tree.*

If it's true, then why can't he remember? And how is it possible the woman knows about it? But deep down he knows it's true. He hasn't wanted to admit it to himself, because Gus is his lifeline.

His *raison d'être.*

If Gus were still alive, he wouldn't be here.

CLAUDIA

AFTER THE OLD man disappears, Claudia stares at the words she has written on the blackboard for a considerable time. Where did they spring from? And what do they mean? The message had come to her the moment the man produced the chalk, and nothing could have stopped her from writing it. She runs a hand through her hair over and over again, thinking how cold the words seem, how matter-of-fact. The man has suffered a loss, no doubt about it, and she has added to his distress. She remains in quiet contemplation, piecing together the clues. A dog, perhaps? Is this the reason he keeps throwing food on the floor? But in what way is the message a lesson? She'd been looking forward to being taught something new, but the whole scenario has been so disappointing.

> *When the lesson has been learned, you may wipe the slate clean.*

Those were the words written on the board when they'd entered the room.

The girl is still asleep. A constant trickle of saliva and snot have formed a small pool on the desk. Why on earth is she so sleepy? It isn't as if she's been up partying all night. As far as Claudia is aware, the house has no other guests, and she'd have heard if there'd been a commotion. It has to be drugs. Drugs or alcohol, but she'd have noticed if the girl had arrived carrying alcohol. Drugs it is then. What a sorry state to be in. To think she'd roped the old man into dragging her all this way, and for nothing. What a waste of effort. She hopes tomorrow's lesson will be more inspiring, or less upsetting at least.

What business is it of yours, Claudia? Let her take as many drugs as she likes. Let him wander the house in dirty clothes and throw food on the floor if that's what he wants. It's none of your goddamn business. The voice in her head is condescending, mocking her efforts. *Always trying to please, that's the trouble with you.*

She massages her forehead in an attempt to loosen the knots that have formed. Her chin quivers; tears sting her eyes. She pushes back her chair and approaches the blackboard on legs that belong to a baby deer. She holds the cloth in her hand, remnants of chalk forming a rainbow on her sweaty palm, and scrubs at the words. Chalk particles from the cloth dance in a beam of sunlight, but the message remains as fresh as the moment she'd written it. Claudia stares in disbelief and tries again. Beneath the message she writes her name, then wipes it away with one swift swipe. She looks at the chalk, certain she'd used the same piece to write the message. How is such a thing possible?

The girl moans in her sleep, restless. It will be impossible for Claudia to drag her up two flights of stairs without the help of the man. She wanders over to the bay window. There he is, at the far end of the garden, perched on a bench. Poor thing. His whole demeanor is forlorn. Her stomach ripples with something akin to guilt. An empty chasm lurks there, too. She isn't ready to feel. Not yet.

Perhaps only he can remove the message on the blackboard.

When the lesson has been learned, you may wipe the slate clean.

She needs something to distract her. Her mind is fraught, her nerves frazzled. Something dark has taken up residence inside her heart and refuses to relinquish its grip. Reading her thoughts, the darkness squeezes hard. A fist of pain courses through her veins, culminating in a vice-like grip in her chest. When the pain subsides, she wanders over to the bookcases, hoping to find something of interest, something to comfort her.

Chalk-dry fingers trace a row of spines. They come to rest on a tatty hardcover, duck-egg blue, with embossed gold lettering. *The Wind in the Willows*, it says. The dark thing in Claudia's heart grays a little and releases the intensity of its grip. Inserting an index finger in the space above the book, she coaxes it from its resting place. Above the title on the front cover is a gold-embossed illustration of the pipe-playing god, Pan. He sits on the riverbank, a badger and a mole for company. His expression is gleeful. He eyes her sideways, as if he sees into her soul.

She opens the book to the title page and reads the name of the author: Kenneth Grahame. The copy is a first edition, printed in 1908. Claudia holds the paper close to her face, inhaling the organic scent of wood pulp, with a hint of vanilla.

Cosseting the book beneath her sweatshirt, she leaves the sleeping girl and returns to her room.

CLAUDIA IS UNSURPRISED to discover she's alone during lunch, and what's more, she is glad, because she has brought *The Wind in the Willows* with her.

Chapter Seven: The Piper at the Gates of Dawn

The macaroni and cheese curdles as she reads, grows cold before she can take a mouthful. No scolding voice to reprimand her for bringing a rare first edition to the table. Claudia reads of a missing otter child, of the moon escaping its moorings to swing clear of the horizon. She feels this line in her heart and in her soul. The night sky, the silver ball, rising above the world to journey wherever it wishes. The moon is its own mistress. It kowtows to no one. What a view of the world it must have from up there.

And then she reads of the terrifying presence of the great god Pan and how his otherwordly music lures the Mole and the Rat onto an island. The great god blesses them with the gift of forgetfulness while leaving nothing but the young otter and hoof prints in the grass. Ratty and Mole are certain they have experienced something elusive.

Claudia pauses her reading to consider her current situation. Why is she here? Is she, too, searching for something? Lunch is a congealed yellow lump, a grumble of maggots left in the sun. She closes the book and studies the cover. The great god Pan winks. "I know what you've done," he says, his breath a ghost's whisper. "But you still have a chance to right the wrong."

STACEY

WHEN STACEY EVENTUALLY wakes, the light has dimmed, and she has no idea what time or even what day it is. She has neither the energy nor the will to care, because the whole of her body is on fire. A throbbing soreness envelops her in its sticky arms, refusing to let go. Her eyes burn, nose runs, and a stinging sensation prickles the entire surface of her skin, as if she had rolled in a clump of nettles.

Hot yet shivering, she opens her eyes and tries to take in her surroundings. She's in a library, she thinks, or an old-fashioned schoolroom—the kind of room rich kids learn in. How did she get here? Apart from the ticking clock, the room is silent. She sits up and yawns, too weak to stand.

The large bay window throws a beam in her direction, making her squint. Fuck, even the light hurts. The spiral staircase in the far corner winds up and up, all the way to the stars. A sign at the bottom of the stairs reads, *First Floor—Non-fiction*, whatever that means. It's dark up there, and she couldn't climb it even if she wanted to.

"Oh, man!" she mutters, patting the pocket of her jacket. A wash of anxiety swells in her chest as she fails to detect her stash. Her fingers fumble at the inner pocket but return empty. Panic makes her focus. She'd been in her room, and now she's here. Therefore, her stash has to be in her room, unless someone's stolen it. But then she remembers: there's nothing to steal because she used what was left the night before. "Fuuuck!"

As things come into focus, she sees the sweet jar. Her stomach heaves at the thought of eating sweets—or any kind of food, for that matter—but she's so thirsty she could drink an entire river. She needs to make it to her room so she can drink from the tap.

Dragging herself to her feet, she sees the board. The board is of little consequence, but the words written on it spark a gram of interest.

> *Gus is dead. You buried him in the garden, beneath the dogwood tree, because the dogwood represents loyalty, and Gus was the most loyal friend you ever had.*

Is Gus a dog? Perhaps not. Perhaps Gus is a person. She pictures the old guy, knee deep in earth, burying a body. She's certain the words were intended for the old guy, but cannot explain why. Perhaps he's a murderer. Cool!

The energy she donates to this thinking makes her nauseous, so she slumps back down on the chair, wraps her arms round her middle, and rocks.

When the wave of nausea subsides, she fumbles in her pocket for her mobile, but it, too, is missing. Pushing against the desk, she stands again. Her legs are gelatinous tentacles that belong to a different kind of creature altogether.

Using the furniture as walking aids, she stumbles over to the chalkboard, picks up the cloth, and scrubs at the words. She wants to replace them with the message FUCK YOU, but the words refuse to budge. She clears her throat, manages to produce a trickle of saliva from the dry muscular tube, then spits on the cloth and tries again. Nothing. Each word, each letter, is as clear as day. She picks up the pale-green chalk that has been left on the shelf and instead scrawls the words on the heavily flocked maroon wallpaper above the fireplace.

FUCK YOU!

She is disappointed by how faint the words look. Pathetic. Barely visible. A sickly pale-green smudge that masks the intent behind them.

Gripping the chalk tight, she repeats the same message in large letters on the teacher's desk before stumbling toward the door.

She makes it as far as the first-floor landing before collapsing in a heap. No way can she reach the second floor. Curled in a ball, she trembles like a dog that's been kicked in the nuts. An acute spasm grips her bowels. If she doesn't get to her room soon, she'll shit herself. Dragging herself onto all fours, she lifts her head in an attempt to establish exactly where she is. The first floor landing stretches ahead of her. High ceiling, deep skirting boards, patterned carpet, and dark doors on either side that seem to shrink into the distance. The name *Danny Torrance* rests on the tip of her tongue, and the image of a kid riding a tricycle looms large, though she cannot pinpoint the reason.

On hands and knees, she crawls up the second flight of stairs and makes it to the bathroom seconds too late.

She feels the wet warmth before she has time to unzip her jeans. The stink of shit burns her nose and makes her vomit. Head in the pan, she purges herself, then lies sprawled on the bathroom floor. Body fluids seep from every orifice: piss, shit, sick. Eyes caked with mucus, nose a dripping tap. Stacey knows beyond a shadow of a doubt that there is only one cure for this, and that cure is not currently available, unless she can find a way to escape this hellhole.

HOWARD

THOUGH THE WORDS on the blackboard have knocked the wind out of his sails, Howard can no longer deny them. He fumbles in the pocket of his joggers in the frail hope that the single hair might magically appear and reignite his dream of resurrecting his beloved pet. The yearning is a physical void in the darkness.

He was so sure Gus had arrived with him. He'd fed him, walked him upon these very grounds. Howard closes his eyes and tries to picture Gus at his side. He leans down and pats thin air, the absence of flesh palpable. Filled with longing, he stands and retraces his steps indoors.

Wanting to be alone, he tiptoes through the hall. He notices the door marked *Library* is ajar, but he ignores it and climbs the stairs to his room. He is still processing the lesson, and is not yet ready to clean the slate.

Howard lies on the bed, exhausted and heartbroken. This grief feels like an illness, one that weakens him to such a point that he believes he is close to death. A single poke from someone's finger is all it will take to push him over the edge of the cliff.

He closes his eyes and drifts, allows his body to tumble down the rocky bank and into the waiting arms of the sea. It's not so bad after all, death. Waves lift him up and carry him farther and farther from shore. Gulls screech overhead, seeming to find the whole thing amusing.

He's sinking now. Down he goes, all the way to the bottom. Cuttlefish and crabs, seahorse and starfish, a host of coral that creates a safe haven for the creatures that live in its depths. No pain, no fear, if he'd known how peaceful it was, he'd have conceded sooner.

A turtle swims past, awarding him no more than a cursory glance, and there in the distance he sees—

Howard is startled awake by someone hammering at the door. Before he has a chance to surface, the door bursts open, and there stands the woman, pinched lips and pale.

"She's sick. I can't lift her on my own," she says.

"What? Who?"

The woman flaps her hands, impatient. "Come with me."

Howard is exhausted by the time he reaches the top of the second flight of stairs. The woman marches on ahead and opens the door to the girl's room without knocking. He gathers his breath, then follows. One glance is all it takes to realize the problem. The girl lies on the bathroom floor, covered in her own filth.

"Thief!" she mumbles as she gains consciousness. The tiled floor is slick with fluids, the stench a physical assault.

"Help me lift her," the woman says to Howard, who cowers in the doorway, reluctant to enter.

"Leave me," the girl mumbles, curling into a ball like an armadillo.

Howard and the woman grapple until they have her precariously balanced on the edge of the tub, then the woman dismisses him with a flick of the wrist.

Howard closes the door behind him, trapping the stench inside.

HAVING SKIPPED LUNCH, Howard feels light-headed. With any luck, there will be coffee and cookies in the dining room. No point in going back to bed. He won't be able to sleep after being so rudely awaken.

Upon entering the hall, he sees that the door to the library still yawns wide, and then discovers that the door to the dining room is locked. It's never locked. He rattles the door knob just to be certain, then turns to face the door marked *Library*. Howard hesitates at the threshold before entering. The clock on the wall beats a rhythm half the speed of his heart. The room is lamplit. Heavy drapes shut out the twilight and anyone with prying eyes who might happen to be in the garden. He breathes in his surroundings. The smell of polish and old wood—the scent of learning. The aura awakens in Howard a sense of familiarity as comfortable as one's own bed.

Even now, after spending several hours coming to terms with the inevitable, he prays for a miracle. He looks to the blackboard, wishing the words have been erased—or better still, that they never existed—but in the dimness, they seem to glow brighter. A luminous, sickly green message eradicates every last speck of hope.

> *Gus is dead. You buried him in the garden, beneath the dogwood tree, because the dogwood represents loyalty, and Gus was the most loyal friend you ever had.*

Howard closes the library door, lessening the risk of unwanted company, and sits at the same desk he sat at earlier. The offending chalk is missing from the shelf. He remembers how after having written the message, the woman had rubbed her hands together with a satisfying sweep before banging it down on the shelf. Someone has used it since. Or moved it.

He sits a while longer, unable to persuade himself to erase the words from the board because he knows that if he does he must promise to pick up the scraps of his life and start over. Without Gus. In a world in which Gus is no more than a memory. Either that, or he must end it. The choice is his.

His back aches. His shoulder throbs. Eventually he gets to his feet and approaches the blackboard with tentative steps. The words written thereon are his opponent, ready to do battle. On the teacher's desk, someone has written a message in green chalk. There it looms, large as life.

FUCK YOU!

Howard flinches at the profanity, unused to such abrasive displays. It had to be the girl. He picks up the cloth and cleans the filth from the desk before turning to face the blackboard. The cloth warms in his hand, but his raised arm is frozen. A lump of gristle forms in his throat, leaving him unable to swallow. He pictures Gus's expression, dark eyes full of trust. He hears the thud of the dog's tail against the wooden floor as it wags contentedly. Then he raises his arm.

"I will never forget you," he whispers in a voice choked and hoarse.

As he wipes the words from the board, specks of dust rise in the air. Dust that smells of wet dog and love.

And with a sweep of the hand, the slate is wiped clean.

HOWARD STANDS IN front of a blackboard, in a room that resembles a library. In his hand he holds a chalk-choked cloth, though he has no idea what it's doing there. The clock on the wall says eight-thirty, and his stomach growls. He shuffles from the room, closing the door behind him, and goes in search of food.

The door marked *Dining Room* is open, and the aroma of freshly brewed coffee wafts from within. Coffee and something sweeter. Howard's mouth waters. On the sideboard next to the carafe is a plate of Danish pastries, the miniature kind, filled with custard, flaked almonds, and a variety of fruit compotes. He pours a cup of coffee and selects a blackberry pastry, devouring it in one mouthful. He thinks about taking a second, but the stench of the girl seems to have followed him. He sniffs the sleeve of his fleece, hoping it might smell of laundry powder, but instead he is met with a stale smell. Body odor and something familiar. Something his olfactory system refuses to name. He should shower and change. Afterward, he will return to the dining room, sit and read a newspaper, and devour a few more pastries.

HIS ROOM WELCOMES him with warmth and soft lighting as he steps out of the bathroom, freshly showered. Folded neatly on the bed is a fresh pair of joggers and a matching top, both in pale gray. A replica of those he has just discarded. A clean pair of slippers wait at the foot of the bed. He dresses quickly, eager to return to the dining room.

As he is about to leave, he sees reflected in the mirror above the old-fashioned chest of drawers an item that has been placed on his bedside cabinet. An item he is certain wasn't there earlier. He hesitates, but then curiosity gets the best of him.

In front of the lamp is a framed photograph. He picks it up and holds it toward the light. It's a photo of a dog, a golden retriever to be precise. Long hair, proud stance, and a face like a teddy bear. *Gus.* The name springs to mind in an instant, and Howard is filled with warmth. The dog belonged to him once, he is certain, though he cannot remember how long ago.

All he knows is they loved each other very much.

He strokes the dog's coat through the glass, sensing its warmth, then replaces the photo on the bedside cabinet and heads back downstairs.

CLAUDIA

CLAUDIA STRIPS THE girl of her clothing, methodical, without sentimentality. She is surprised to see the girl cry. Swollen tears roll silently down prominent cheekbones to form a puddle in the dip between her clavicles.

"Jesus, what a mess!" Claudia eases her into the tub then turns on the shower, lets the flow of water run over her body and hair before shampooing and washing her with bath gel that smells of a lemon grove. The cobra tattoo on the girl's arm spits and hisses, but the sound is lost to the force of the spray. All the while, her tears continue to fall. They mingle with the water from the shower head, so Claudia is none-the-wiser. The girl's body trembles, and her teeth chatter, but Claudia has expert hands. She does not speak as she pats her dry. Instead, she lets her actions do the talking. She bundles the soiled clothes into a polythene laundry bag and ties the top tight. All except the leather jacket, which is salvageable.

"These need burning. Do you understand?"

The girl does not answer.

"I'll find a bin and set fire to them. It's not fair to expect others to wash that shit out." Her manner is abrupt, though not unkind. Matter-of-fact; no more, no less.

Wrapped in a towel, the girl sits on the lid of the toilet seat as Claudia combs her hair with a wide-toothed comb and a mother's touch. When she disappears into the bedroom and returns with her arms full of pale gray fleece, the girl does not protest. Too weak, too spent. She allows Claudia to dress her in the uniform with little more than a sniff and a sob. Now they look the same, like mother and daughter—almost.

Claudia helps the girl into the bedroom, hands her a glass of water, and supports her head as the girl takes tiny sips.

"My phone. Can you find it for me?"

Claudia gives a cursory glance around the room, then shakes her head. "It's not here. Nothing we think we need is here. Only what is good for us."

"You don't understand. I need help. I'll die otherwise." Her voice is fragile, taut, a delicate membrane on the point of snapping.

Claudia looks her in the eye, then takes a deep breath. "I'll help you, but not in the way you want." She takes hold of the girl's hand, tracing prominent veins with a hangnailed index finger.

The cobra on the girl's arm flares its hood, tastes the air with a forked tongue, and spits a stream of abuse in the woman's face.

CLAUDIA SITS IN the wingback chair beside the girl's bed all night long. During the rare moments the girl sleeps, she dozes, but remains attuned to the girl's breathing. Half the night is spent mopping her brow or helping her to the bathroom when stomach spasms bend her double. There seems no end to the amount of bodily fluid she produces. Shit, piss, vomit, sweat, mucus—the whole gamut. And then there's the pleading, the trembling, the constant yawning.

Worst of all are the hallucinations.

Claudia has no idea which drugs the girl has taken, but she understands the process of withdrawal. The physical symptoms she can cope with, the psychological less so. At times, the girl writhes in agony, clutching her temples and moaning, but it's the scratching that threatens to break her. In the early hours of the morning, she starts clawing at her chest. Next it's her arms and legs, then scalp. She frets about being covered in bugs, becoming more and more agitated as the night wears on. Black bugs with red stripes, she says, flicking them off her body, time and time again. The term *delusional parasitosis* buzzes in Claudia's head, growing silver wings that threaten to take flight. She dampens its spirit with an imaginary swipe of calamine because she cannot remember what the term means.

Claudia bathes the girl's body with cool flannels, takes nail scissors and cuts her fingernails to the quick to prevent her scratches from breaking the skin. A few nails still wear a daub of black polish near the cuticle. The skin beneath the nail tip is red and sore, as if it has been gouged. Claudia promises the girl she will give her a manicure once she feels better. "Black polish with silver moons," she says.

DAWN LIGHTENS THE floral curtains, reviving peonies and dahlia, poppies and clematis, though not yet giving them permission to display their color. The girl is asleep, so Claudia tiptoes from the room, descends a flight of stairs to where her own room awaits, and takes a shower. As she dries, she looks in the mirror. The bruises around her neck have faded to green, which means the healing process is beginning to take place. *The hemoglobin has morphed into biliverdin.* This snippet of knowledge elbows its way out of her neocortex of its own accord, though she cannot recall having put it in there to begin with. The bruises are now less sore to touch, but when she puts on the clean jogging suit, she still makes sure they are covered.

The Wind in the Willows remains on her bedside cabinet, a folded tissue marking her page. She has read it from cover to cover twice, and is on the third round. It has provided a temporary escape from the gloom.

At 07:30 she returns to the girl's bedroom, hoping to persuade her to eat some breakfast. She needs to replenish her strength, but it will not be easy, especially if the vomiting phase is not over.

She enters without knocking, acknowledging for the first time that the bedrooms are not lockable. The waft of a sickroom greets her—sour, acidic, yeasty, with an undercurrent of bleach that sends Claudia's mind reeling. The bed is empty bed. All crumpled sheets and flattened pillows. Claudia's heart skips a beat, but then she hears a tap running in the bathroom. She knocks on the bathroom door even though it isn't locked.

"You all right in there?"

A muttered reply, followed by a spit. "Fine," though it sounds like *swine*. The girl is cleaning her teeth. A positive sign.

Claudia opens the curtains and window to allow daylight and fresh air to enter. The impression of the girl's body is a ghost on the mattress, and for the first time,

Claudia feels a throb of sympathy. Since arriving at the house on Lacelean Street, she has felt empty, like a barrel of air, the only connection to her emotional psyche delivered in the form of a fictional mother otter, her only pulse of fear piqued by the illustrated god Pan, who claims to know what it is she has done, even though she doesn't know herself.

The sound of a toilet flushing lets her know that the girl is almost finished in the bathroom, so she quickly tidies the bed in hopes that a tidy bed will deter the girl from wanting to climb back in. As she straightens the sheets, she sees it, a desiccated bug—six legs, large thorax, black abdomen with horizontal red stripes—just like the girl had said.

The bathroom door opens, and Claudia flicks the dead bug with a thumbnail. In mid-air, it springs to life, and silver wings unfold. With a click-clack buzzing sound, it takes to the air and soars out the window.

Flustered, Claudia takes a deep breath and prepares to face the girl. "How are you feeling?" Her lips twitch as she drinks in the girl's ghostly complexion, her sunken eyes, her waif-like gait. Claudia believes that if she were to blow in the girl's direction, she would break into seeds and scatter in the breeze.

The girl's footsteps are silent as she approaches the bed. "Was it you?" Her voice is a dry whisper.

"I beg your pardon?"

"Here. In this room. Did you stay with me last night?"

Claudia nods and looks down at her feet, suddenly embarrassed by the intimacy she shared with this stranger. "Will you come to breakfast, or shall I bring you something?"

"I—I couldn't." The girl sits on the edge of bed, her body turned away from Claudia.

"Then I'll bring you something. You must eat."

AT TEN MINUTES to nine, Claudia plays her trump card. "Feel up to coming downstairs? A stretch of the legs will do you good."

The girl sits in the wingback chair, dressed in a clean jogging suit. She has nibbled at a slice of toast and drunk half a cup of tea.

"It's raining," she says. The view from the window agrees with her. The garden wears a shroud of gray to match their jogging suits. Claudia thinks that if they were to go outside they would become invisible, which might not be as bad as it sounds.

She has no intention of going outside, though. What she really wants is for all of them to descend on the library so that they may receive their second lesson. She is obsessed with the library and the lessons. The fluttering sensation that lurks at the very core of her being tells her that the library is the reason they are all here. The other two do not seem to have caught on yet.

"A book then? Do you read? It might help take your mind off things." She is skating on thin ice, wary of it forming a crack into which one or other of them might plunge, never to be seen again.

The girl scowls. Her left leg is crossed over the right. It bounces constantly. ADHD, Claudia thinks, though it might just be the girl's body preparing to deal with an anticipated threat. When she speaks, her voice is a metal rasp, corroded with rust. "I read a Stephen King book once. Something about a rabid dog." She sniffs. "Is it true that rabies makes you afraid of water? I mean, what the fuck?"

"I believe the fear of water has something to do with throat spasms. Rabies makes swallowing difficult." Claudia tries to smile, but her lips refuse to cooperate. She does not think they'll find books by Stephen King in the library, but if she can persuade the girl of the possibility, she might get her to come with her. "Let's go to library and see if they have any books on the subject, shall we?" She holds out a hand, and with some hesitancy, the girl takes it.

THE OLD MAN waits in the hallway, his hand on the library door knob, ready to turn it the moment the others arrive. He sighs with relief as they descend. Claudia is glad to see him, especially as he was absent during breakfast. The apples of his cheeks shine. He is clean-shaven, and he appears to have cut his own hair. No food stains color his sweatshirt. No smell of unwashed skin or wet dog follows him.

The first thing Claudia notices as she enters the library is the blackboard. She wonders who wiped away the message she had written the previous day. The old man? The girl? An elusive teacher? She assumes it's the man, because she is convinced that only the person to whom the message applies can remove it. Today she feels full of trepidation in case she is next, and yet at the same time, she is eager to get on with it. Get it over with. An itch that must be scratched.

The walk downstairs has exhausted the girl. She slumps at her desk, legs sprawled and head lolled to one side. Claudia worries she might leave at any moment, as her demeanor is one of utter boredom. The jars of chalk remain on all three desks, just as they left them. Once all three of them are seated, Claudia removes the lid from her jar and chooses a chalk in the palest of pinks. Instinct warns her that today's lesson will be directed at her, so she hopes that in choosing this color, its message will be gentle.

At the corner of her eye, she senses movement. The girl has stood, and Claudia's heart skips a beat. She would do anything to prevent her from leaving, so she reminds her about the books. "Stephen King." She manages a wink, then nods in the direction of the bookcases that encircle the room. "They're in alphabetical order, according to the author's surname. Starting with *A* over there." She points behind her. All three of them need to be in this room for this to work. She feels it in her gut.

Claudia breathes a sigh of relief when the girl wanders over to the bookshelves and begins to browse. The girl is tense, though. Every move she makes is like the twang of an overtightened guitar string. Just so long as she doesn't snap, Claudia thinks. Not yet, anyway.

She turns her attention back to the stub of chalk, grips it tight between her thumb and two fingers, as though about to apply lipstick, then passes it to the old man. Perhaps he will seek revenge for the scandalous words she wrote the previous day. But to do so, he would need to know something of her past. Something personal. Something even she has forgotten. The same way she inexplicably knew a secret about him.

He stares at the chalk in the palm of his hand as if it is an object of great mystery, a thing he does not know how to use. It lies there, nestled among cracked skin and sweat, until he shakes his head and issues a desperate groan.

"Hah! Fucking ace!"

The girl's voice startles them both, and the man drops the chalk. It rolls down the slope of the desk and comes to rest at his swollen, slippered feet.

"I can't reach," he says, turning to Claudia in despair.

The girl returns to her desk, slaps down a hardback copy of Stephen King's *It*, and says. "I've seen the movie. There's this freaking clown, right, and he lives in the sewer—"

The man interrupts her. "Pick it up, will you? Young bones and all that." He points at the chalk, and she does as he asks. The tone of his voice is haughtier today, more self-assured, Claudia notices.

She senses the moment it happens, sees the change in the girl's body as well as in her face the moment she touches the chalk. The girl twitches, as if she has witnessed something bad, then steps up to the blackboard and begins to write.

STACEY

YOU SKEWERED KEVIN'S *windpipe with the flat head screwdriver he'd been using to tighten the handle of the kitchen cabinet, leaving him to drown in his own blood. Kevin was NOT the most loyal friend you ever had. In fact, he was an utter bastard.*

Stacey takes two steps back, mouthing the words her hand has just written, as though seeing them for the first time. "Woah!" she says, grinning. She turns to face Claudia and raises the offending hand in the air, ready to strike a high five. "Cool! You! A murderer! Who'd have guessed?"

Seeing the horror on Claudia's face, her enthusiasm wanes. Claudia leans forward, gripping the farthest edge of the desk. White knuckles, sickly pallor. Her mouth is an elongated *O* shape, from which rapid breaths stutter.

Stacey stands frozen, unsure of how to react or what to say next. She glances at the old man who looks equally aghast, then turns once more to face the board. Her right fist clutches the stick of chalk, while the left fist clenches and unclenches repeatedly. A momentary pause, then beneath the previous message, she writes:

STACEY WOZ ERE!

The letters loom large. She encircles them with a crudely drawn heart, elongating the point of the heart into a forked devil's tail. To the curves of the heart, she adds devil horns. To each side, she adds feathered wings. All the while, the tip of her tongue pokes out from between her teeth, as focused on the task as she is.

Graffiti complete, she replaces the chalk on Claudia's desk without so much as a glance, picks up the Stephen King book, and staggers from the room.

She barely makes it to the corridor before a torrent of watery yellow bile, with morsels of undigested toast dotted here and there, spatters the carpet. The lurid pattern wears it well, the greens and browns acting as an impressive disguise—the plain wallpaper less so. Stephen King's *It* survives the ordeal when it gets flung across the landing.

Stacey bends double, gathering her breath. She feels like shit, and is so desperate for a fix, she considers the possibility of getting hold of an inhalant—some paint thinner from one of the garden sheds, perhaps. The woman had promised her a manicure, therefore she must have found some nail polish remover. Christ, cold turkey is torture. She's been offered nothing since she got here. No sign of alcohol or a smoke anywhere. No methadone or opiate antagonist of any kind. If this is some kind of rehab clinic, she should be given prescription drugs. And where's her fucking mobile? Thieving bastards!

The cobra on her upper arm snakes its way through the neck of her sweatshirt and spits a stream of venom. She watches it mingle with the pool of vomit until it is impossible to tell where the human fluid ends and the reptile's begins.

IN THE SHORT amount of time she has been absent, her room has been refreshed. Clean linen, disinfected bathroom, windows open wide to encourage the smell of roses to enter. There it is again. The same sense of nostalgia she'd experienced in the garden the day after she'd arrived. The day she'd scoped the place for an escape route. At this moment in time, she has neither the energy nor the will to escape, even if it were possible. She craves one thing and one thing only—her next fix.

Having rinsed her mouth in the bathroom, she curls in a ball on the bed, moaning with frustration. Desperation.

She would plead, but there is no one to plead to. Beg, but there is no one to beg. She knows she should grab a towel from the bathroom and mop up the mess in the corridor, but she can't be bothered. They forced her to go cold turkey, so let them clean the mess.

Once the craving subsides, she picks up the book by King and begins to read. A mighty tome, one that makes her wrists ache from holding. She sits up and balances it on her thighs instead.

The very first chapter has her hooked, loosens the narcotic grip and replaces it with a craving of a different kind.

The love and adoration of a younger sibling.

In the book, young George worships his older brother, Bill. There is nothing he won't do for him, yet when Pennywise, the yellow-eyed dancing clown, entices young George with the smell of the carnival and the gift of a balloon, Bill is not there to save him.

You must not take things from strangers, Georgie!

It was Bill who made the paper boat that doomed his brother. Bill who encouraged George to go out and play. Therefore, it is Bill who is responsible when the clown rips off George's arm and kills him.

Why does Stacey bleed tears over the pages? They soak into the paper like vinegar on fish wrap, turning the print to pulp in a matter of seconds. She is unable to read further because the words are a blur. They swim in her vision as though trying to avoid the storm drain. She licks her upper lip—salt and snot, the taste of pain. Held captive within the saline are letters. Letters that line up side by side to form a word, a name—*Lisa*.

She squeezes her eyes tight and holds her breath in an attempt to keep the name and all it encompasses inside her, but the cobra uncoils from her arm, sinks its fangs in the soft skin behind her ear and whispers one word, "*JUDASSS!*" The final consonant is a hiss of spite.

She gasps at the pain, the accusation, and the precious word—*Lisa*—evaporates into thin air.

CLAUDIA

THE OLD MAN is speaking, but his words wash over Claudia like tears at a funeral. A vague awareness of the scrape of his chair against the wooden floor, and the next thing she knows she is all alone.

> *You skewered Kevin's windpipe with the flat head screwdriver he'd been using to tighten the handle of the kitchen cabinet, leaving him to drown in his own blood. Kevin was NOT the most loyal friend you ever had; in fact, he was an utter bastard.*

Kevin. The hard consonant at the front of the word is a kick to the ribs. She flinches from the pain. *Kevin, kick your head in.* A phrase she associates with his name. Words as familiar as her reflection.

> *Kevin was NOT the most loyal friend you ever had…*

She considers this phrase for several moments, confused at first, but then it dawns. Kevin was not her friend at all. He was her husband. Or rather he *is* her husband.

You skewered Kevin's windpipe with the flat head screwdriver…leaving him to drown in his own blood.

Has she *murdered* him? Her own husband? The words imply as much, but Jesus Christ, she has no recollection of the incident. A cold sweat snakes a trail between her breasts. Her hands tingle as though wired to an electric current. *Think, Claudia, think!*

She pictures the clothes she arrived in: black leggings, cheap, with sagging knees. She'd peeled them off in the bathroom on arrival. Surely there'd have been blood? She studies the insides of her wrists. The bruising has faded, but it's still possible to make out the shape of a man's thumbprint. Larger than hers and pale green. The kind of imprint The Incredible Hulk might leave behind. *Don't make me angry. You wouldn't like me when I'm angry.* Too late, mate. Kevin's face swims in her vision. Handsome, once upon a time, but his temper made him ugly, both inside and out.

What else was she wearing when she arrived? She massages the bridge of her nose and tries to focus. A mint-green shirt, buttoned down the front. No blood, though. She's certain. The knot in her stomach loosens a little.

But the dried-up inkwell in the corner of the desk suggests otherwise. It issues a throaty gurgle, followed by a volcanic eruption of blood that sprays her face, spatters the pale-gray sweatshirt, and runs down her white-knuckled hands in red ribbons.

Claudia scrabbles to her feet, knocking the chair to the floor. It lies there, prone, legs splayed and back broken. The bloody eruption has stopped now, but the desk is soaked, as is the wooden floor beneath it. Hit by something from behind, she turns abruptly. On the floor lies a crumpled piece of fabric. She stoops to pick it up. A lemon-colored T-shirt, the image of a huge slice of watermelon on the front. A red grin and seeds like rotten teeth. It is covered in dried blood, as if it has bitten its victim straight through the jugular. She holds it in both hands and stares at the stain. Holds it to her nose and inhales the chemical tang of bleach. The memory is sharp, as sudden as the T-shirt striking her back, and she knows she was wearing this garment when she attacked him.

She remembers the whoosh of air as his trachea punctured, and how the force of the blow knocked her sideways. He collapsed in a heap—eyes on stalks—comical if it wasn't so tragic. The screwdriver projected from his throat, its red handle disguised by the blood that oozed from between his fingers as he tried to pull it out.

The slice of melon widens its grin with each and every detail she remembers, until the corners of its mouth can stretch no further. It will swallow her soon, gobble her up in one mouthful.

Claudia does not stop to consider how the soiled T-shirt got here because all she can think about right now is one word: *MURDERER!* Three syllables, each spilling into the next. She scrunches the T-shirt into a ball, desperate to hide the evidence of her guilt, then collapses onto the old man's chair. Hers lies sprawled on the ground, just as she left it, and for a moment, she thinks she sees Kevin's body lying there instead, his pallor as gray as her clothing, lips blue and eyes glazed. She blinks, and he is gone.

Panic seizes her by the throat, threatens to strangle her as his hands had done on more than one occasion. She must confess what she has done. She must get help. He might still be alive. Claudia tries to count how many days she has been at the house on Lacelean Street but finds it impossible. They have blended into one another, like custard on unset jelly. Bloodstained T-shirt in hand, she rushes from the room on legs that threaten to crumple.

Claudia tries every door knob on the ground floor but finds them all locked. She bangs on the door marked *Kitchen*, screams for help. But she is shouting into the void. She must get to a telephone and call the police. Surely there must be a phone somewhere? She remembers the girl asking for her mobile. Remembers how she had cut her off and told her she didn't need it. Something tells her the old man doesn't have one either. In that case, she must find someone who does.

A desperate whimper accompanies her as she runs out of the house and heads for the gate. The T-shirt is wrung again and again in her hands, as if she is trying to squeeze out the days'-old blood. And why does it smell of bleach? *Because you wore it while cleaning up the mess, Claudia.* She reaches the gate and pulls. It rattles but refuses to open. She tries again, but the metal clangs in protest at its rough treatment. The gate is locked. Firmly and securely bolted. No way out, no way in. She slumps to her knees and sobs.

She does not hear his footsteps, despite the gravel. Claudia opens her eyes to see a dark shadow looming over her. They've come for me, she thinks, but it is just the old man.

"Claudia?"

Hearing her name spoken for the first time in days feels strange. She had almost forgotten it.

He holds out a hand and helps her to her feet.

Her face is a mess—hot, sweating, sticky with snot. She unravels the T-shirt and points to the stain. "I—I killed him!"

She studies his face, as he studies hers. White hairs that protrude from his nose flutter as he breathes. "Kevin?"

She nods. "My husband."

He pauses. "Are you sure?"

"Of course I'm sure." Her voice is a snapping twig. "Kevin Richards." She frowns, confused by the name she has spoken. If she married him, then why isn't she called Claudia Richards? The label on the jar of chalks swims in her vision—*Claudia Dance*. She knew someone named Claudia Dance once. Such a happy girl. A girl with ambition. A girl who aspired to dance in the theatre, just as her birth name predicted. But this is not who she has become.

She whispers the other name, trying it on for size, "Claudia Richards." It feels familiar on her tongue, the rolling flow of it. She doesn't like Claudia Richards, though. Claudia Richards is as different to Claudia Dance as one could get.

"I mean, are you certain you killed him?"

She waves the T-shirt in front of his face, eyes wild, animalistic. "Blood!"

"Yes, but blood does not necessarily mean he's dead now, does it?" His accent is haughty. Superior. Not the sniveling weakling he seemed when they first met.

His words make no sense, so she dismisses them. She's as guilty as the words on the blackboard suggest. "I need to get to a phone. I need to call the police. An ambulance. Anyone!" She points toward the gate, and her face crumples. "They've locked the frigging gate!" Claudia rarely swears. She is used to keeping her tongue at bay, in case of retaliation, so her outburst comes as a shock to her ears.

The old man's expression remains as calm as a placid lake on a summer's day. "What address would you give?"

"Address?"

"Yes…Where does Kevin live?" His eyes are wise. In the flecks of blue, Claudia sees specks of knowledge that she does not yet possess. She opens her mouth to speak but cannot find the words. She has no idea where she and Kevin lived prior to her arrival at Lacelean Street. No house number, no street name, not even a town.

Howard understands all of this, because he has been in her position. Blind. "You see?" he says. "Phoning the police is not the answer." He stabs a finger in the direction of the house. "The answer lies in there."

Claudia feels a wave of calm spread from her toes to her forehead. Warm, comforting. He holds out a hand, and she passes him the bloodstained T-shirt. His slippered feet crunch softly as he walks away, fading to nothing. She waits for him to disappear, then follows suit.

HOWARD

HE HADN'T BEEN able to bear it back in the library. The words of condemnation. The look of utter despair on her face. So he'd taken the coward's way out and had left her there, alone. Her face had brought back all the feelings he'd had when she'd written the message about Gus, and he couldn't deal with it.

In his mind, he revisits the scene. The chalk she'd passed him had grown warm in his hand. So warm, in fact, that he'd dropped it in case it burned him. He hadn't known what to write, had no interest in revenge, and until the girl named Stacey had picked up the chalk, he didn't know which of them would be next. It could easily have been his turn again, because he knows there's more that needs to be uncovered about his past. So much more. He senses it wriggling inside him. A worm-like thing, pus-filled and angry. It squirms inside his intestines, taking little nibbles at his bowel as it journeys south. He hopes he will shit it out soon. Be done with it.

From the garden bench, the bench where only two days ago he'd been certain Gus lay at his feet, he'd watched her flee the house and run toward the gate. He'd waited a while, his own heart attempting to escape through his ribcage, but when she'd slumped to her knees, he knew he had to go to her aid.

He'd done his best to placate her, knowing that even if it were possible, escape was not the answer. She needed to stay and face her demons, just as he did. Accepting the death of Gus and erasing the message on the board had brought him one step closer. Nothing more, nothing less. If he could help her and the girl, he would.

HOWARD HOVERS ABOUT in the hallway, uncertain of what to do next. He knows she follows close behind, so he leaves the front door open. The door to the library reveals a crack a few inches wide, sufficient to see that the incriminating words remain on the board.

All the other doors are firmly closed. Locked, too, he imagines—at least until coffee time. Claudia's feet crunch up the gravel drive, her pace slow and reluctant. He does not want to be in the hall when she arrives, nor does he intend to enter the library. Without turning around, he climbs the stairs as quickly as possible. *How old are you, Howard?* The answer lies snuggled in his heart, somewhere between the aorta and pulmonary artery if the little stab of pain is anything to go by.

His room on the first floor feels cold and alien. It smells of polish and fresh linen, not wet dog and stale food. The bed is made, the bathroom cleaned. Damask drapes flutter in the breeze from an open window. Howard leans in the window and takes in the view. A wide courtyard, laid with original diamond-paved bricks. A stable block with arched windows and door. How has he not noticed this until now? Too wrapped up in his own misery to care, he assumes. The sight of the stables sends a shiver down his spine. A pleasurable shiver, one linked to good memories buried deep. While he cannot pinpoint them, he knows they are good because they taste nutty and sweet, like malted-milk cookies.

Footsteps prowl above his head. Restless footsteps, agitated. He thinks back to when Claudia had called on him for help. He retraces his steps up the second flight of stairs and all the way along the landing to the farthest end. Stacey's room. He pictures her there. A caged lion, teeth bared, ready to pounce. Back and forth, back and forth, she prowls. He is thankful she has no access to music, since he imagines it would be blasting right now. Still, the pacing is disturbing enough. It unsettles him. Defaces the pocket-sized book of calm he has managed to acquaint himself with these past two days.

He will go for a walk, that's what he'll do. A walk around the grounds and the courtyard, where he will picture a horse as fine and noble as he can imagine. An American Quarter Horse with a red sorrel coat, sleek mane, and sunny disposition.

HOWARD APPROACHES THE stables with confident steps. A small ménage to the left, one lightly harrowed. The pain in his right shoulder has eased these past few days to such an extent he hardly notices it. His arthritic hip has calmed too. When the horse whinnies, he thinks he imagines it. A trick of the wind, perhaps, or the squeal of a latch. Nevertheless, his stomach does a little jig.

The top half of the stable door is fastened to the wall by means of a wrought-iron cabin hook that rattles in the wind. The sudden appearance of the horse's head forces him to take a step back. Surprise, shock, and so much more. Why he is so surprised to discover a horse in a stable, he does not know. In all likelihood, it's because the horse is the first living creature he has seen since arriving— apart from Claudia and Stacey, of course.

The horse whinnies and thrusts out its head. Almond eyes lock Howard's, and in doing so, a pulse of energy flows between equine and man.

Howard steps closer, grinning from ear to ear. "Well, hello there," he says, his voice gentle, cautious. He holds out a hand, tentative, and the horse nose-bumps his wrist in greeting. The horse's breath warms Howard's skin, and his head nods a familiar rhythm. Between the eyes, slightly off-center, the sorrel coat wears a white patch, the size of a ten-pence coin. Howard leans forward and rubs the white patch with his forehead, and the horse returns the gesture. He recognizes this horse, and the horse recognizes him. No doubt about it.

Howard instinctively delves into the pocket of his gray joggers in search of a peppermint, but finds nothing except a soiled tissue. "Sorry, boy," he whispers. "I'll bring you some next time, I promise."

The horse nickers and snorts, nudging Howard's shoulder as if to say, *I'll hold you to that.*

The sound of a window being prised open draws Howard's attention back to the house. The girl, Stacey, thrusts her head out of the upstairs window and leans on the sill, watching. From where he stands, Howard cannot make out her features, but he's close enough to see that her face is pale, her hair lank and missing the aggressive spikes it once wore. Spikes that shouted, *Keep your distance, or I'll poke you in the eye!*

Howard raises a hand and waves, but she does not wave back, nor does she turn away. The ghost of a girl continues to stare, unflinching.

When he turns back to the horse, he finds it gone. No proud head at the stable door, though the smell of warm hay lingers in the air.

Howard is too afraid to look inside the stable in case his mind has been playing tricks on him again. He does not want that to be the case, because he feels he is starting to turn a corner, opening a door long closed.

Instead, he stands and listens.

No snort, no whinny, not even the sound of breathing. Howard spins on slippered heels and makes his way back to the house with his head bowed low.

STACEY

STACEY CAN READ no further. It's too distressing, and besides, the bugs are back. Beneath her jogging suit, they buzz and scarper, tease and bite until she peels off her clothes and scratches herself raw with what little nail remains after the woman cut them. The itch is unbearable, so she heads to the shower and lets the cool water douse her from head to toe. She dries her face and watches, mesmerized, as the black and red insects swirl down the plughole.

She thinks about the message on the blackboard. The words her own hand had written. When she looks at the hand now, she sees pale skin, bird-like bones, fingernails with fragments of black polish. It does not look capable of such an act. She cannot remember what she wrote, just the first bit:

> *You skewered Kevin's windpipe with the flat head screwdriver...*

The grin still quivers at her chin. Is the woman a murderer? If so, she does a pretty good job of disguising it.

Stacey recalls the night the woman spent at her bedside. A mother in a stranger's body. She tries to remember her real mother but fails. And Lisa. Who is she? She repeats the name again and again. Whispered syllables, a secret yet to be revealed.

Empty, both physically and mentally. Her body is being forced to purge itself beyond her will. It's a remarkable thing, the body. The way in which it will rid itself of intruders and unwanted chemicals given half a chance. The index finger on her right hand points at her, willing herself to remember. A sliver of glass from a jam jar. It had buried itself beneath the skin for several weeks until eventually her body said, *That's enough! You don't belong here!* The sliver of glass had been ousted. Its head had poked through the skin, and she had plucked it from its bed with a tweezer. How can she remember this but not her own mother?

Her stomach growls, hungry, like a lion that has not fed all winter. She prowls the room, back and forth, back and forth, searching, though for what, she does not know. Whatever it is, she won't find it here in this room.

Drawn toward the window by a scuffle in the courtyard, she opens the casement catch and leans out. The old man stands in front of the stables, talking to a horse. His face is in profile, as is the horse's head. They nudge noses, as if they have known one another for a very long time. He seems more alive than he did previously, the man. Cleaner, more alert, posher.

He notices her watching and waves, but she does not wave back. He might call her down, and then what would she do? She's curious, but not enough to take things further. Not yet, anyway. She's lonely, not desperate. The scene has provided a temporary distraction from the internal itch that has overtaken the external one. The internal itch is far worse, far more difficult to scratch.

The scent from the rosebush below her window makes her look down, and by the time she looks up again, the horse has disappeared. Did she imagine it? The man's body language suggests disappointment. His head hangs low. Soon, he turns away from the stable and makes his way toward the house. Stacey closes the window and retreats back to the safety of her bed.

The novel sits on the bedside cabinet, itching to be picked up. With a sigh, she does so, muttering words about how it had better not upset her, before locating chapter two.

It picks up the story twenty-seven years later, with the violent actions of a homophobic gang and the reappearance of the clown beneath the canal bridge. Stacey shifts in the bed, immersed in the characters, yet discomforted by their behavior. Deep inside her, she feels the lives these characters lead, especially the thugs. It's as if she knows them from another time, another place.

She closes the book momentarily, marking the page with her index finger. There are parallels within this fictional world. The gap in time—a *then* and *now*—woven with threads of similarity. A paper boat, a paper hat—both of which ignite a path of destruction. A real carnival, an imaginary carnival. And in both time periods, Pennywise, waiting in the water for Georgie and then Adrian.

She gives this some thought before concluding that there will always be an evil clown waiting to trip you up, no matter how many years pass by. Perhaps it's impossible to escape the inevitable, so why bother trying?

The physical symptoms of addiction have eased these past few hours; the mental craving less so. But she is not addicted, is she? Not really. She could stop anytime she wants. Beneath the sleeve of her fleece, the cobra stirs. *Feed me,* it hisses. *I will not be stilled!* The serpent coils itself tight around her upper arm, so tight she feels her own blood pulse beneath it. Like Cleopatra's bracelet squeezing, *squeezing*. A dull ache, a throb. The cobra spreads its hood and hisses again. Beneath the fleece, Stacey recognizes the shape of its head in the skinny dip between the muscles of the bicep and shoulder. She knows that if it strikes, it could kill her within thirty minutes. It won't, though. It threatens, but it will not strike her dead, because if she dies, it dies with her. Only the rose will remain.

"Fuck you," she hisses back, and the serpent quiets.

Her stomach growls, so she goes to the bathroom, snaps off a single sheet of toilet paper to use as a bookmark, and heads downstairs in search of sustenance.

The old man lounges on an armchair in the dining room, a china cup of coffee on his left and a plate of tiny pastries on his right. A flaky crumb sits on his upper lip, and Stacey's stomach roils.

He puts down a magazine and looks at her, his face a worn map. "How are you today, Stacey?"

She flinches at the mention of her name. It sounds alien to her ears, like it belongs to someone else. She shrugs. "Been better." Turning her back on him, she pours a coffee. Her hands shake, the cup rattles against the saucer. Why can't they put out chunky mugs instead of this poncy nonsense?

Beside the cafetière is a plate of chocolate cookies. Hobnobs, her favorite. She wraps four or five in a paper napkin, picks up the cup, and heads back to her room.

CLAUDIA

THE REIGN OF calm that Howard managed to instill in Claudia lasts until she steps back into the library. Seeing the words on the blackboard sends a ripple of panic—the equivalent of a magnitude 7.0 earthquake—coursing through her veins. The shock wave is seismic, a tsunami of bile in her guts. She approaches the board tentatively, as though it might swallow her whole.

In her left hand, she holds the cloth. In her right, the pale-pink chalk. An image floats in her vision. An image of a girl named Alice, who finds herself falling down a rabbit hole, though she cannot put the image in context. A bottle labeled *Drink me*. A cake with the words *Eat me*, spelled out with currants. What a choice to have to make!

> *When the lesson has been learned you may wipe the slate clean.*

Claudia is not ready to do so. With one swipe, she erases the devilish heart the girl has drawn, then puts down the cloth and raises her arm, an arm that trembles with aftershock.

Beneath the message of condemnation, she writes another.

> *Please, whoever reads this, I beg of you, phone the police. And an ambulance, too. It might not be too late to save him. My husband's name is Kevin Richards, and I think I may have killed him.*
>
> *I am sorry, but I cannot give you any further information.*

As she dots the full stop, the chalk snaps, such is her force. She wipes her sweaty palms down the front of her joggers and steps back, mouthing the words she has added. She issues a desperate moan. The moan of someone trapped inside a nightmare. Surely someone will see it? There are people in this house. People other than her, the old man, and the girl. If there weren't, then how are the rooms kept clean? Who provides their meals?

Claudia stares at the door which she has left ajar, willing someone to enter. Someone with a phone, or at least a compassionate ear. She rights the wooden chair that she toppled earlier. One of the struts at the back is broken, but she doesn't seem to notice. Claudia sits and waits, her face half turned toward the board and half toward the door.

The wall clock ticks away the seconds, and gradually her heart rate slows to match its rhythm. Apart from the clock's heartbeat and her own, the house is as silent as the grave.

No one will come to her rescue. Deep down, she knows this for certain. The battle belongs to her and no one else.

> *When the lesson has been learned you may wipe the slate clean.*

What lesson? She has accepted culpability, yes, but all she has learned in doing so is that it is likely she is a murderer. Is there a word for a woman who murders her husband? It is not matricide. Matricide means to murder one's mother. If there is a word, she cannot think of it. The old man might know. He seems educated, well-spoken. Her opinion of him has changed these past few days. Claudia is sure there is more to him than meets the eye. The unkempt bum who fell from the bus has hidden his light under a bushel.

She thinks back to her first impression of him. The stink, the way he spat phlegm onto the ground, the pathetic sobbing. And yet, the bus had picked him up in front of tall metal gates. She remembers thinking they belonged to a mansion, or a park, not unlike the gates of this house. Might it have been his home?

You need to be more decisive, Claudia, she tells herself. Stop daydreaming and take action. She knows what she will do. She will give it one hour, and if both messages remain on the blackboard, and if by then no police arrive, she will wipe the slate clean.

THE SOUND OF panpipes accompanies Claudia up the stairs, louder and louder, the closer she gets to her room. An exotic tune, bright and whimsical. A tune that conjures an image of a sunlit forest. She pauses at the door, certain the music comes from inside.

She is not mistaken. At the edge of her bed sits the god Pan. He faces the window and does not turn as she enters. His appearance and his music steal her breath. He is magnificent. His music is magnificent.

She enters, closes the door softly behind her. She does not want any of the other guests to hear. She wishes to keep the god Pan to herself. Her secret. All the angst and dread she has felt since arriving at this house—especially today—evaporates. It becomes a visible thing. A vine of ivy, laced with silver thread, that drizzles from her pores, her ears, her mouth, and drifts toward his fingers. Pan absorbs the angst and makes it his own, turning each heart-shaped leaf into a sweet note that tastes of ripe peaches, the first breath of a newborn lamb, the scent of pine needles on freshly fallen snow.

There remains the tiniest scrap of mistrust. How can this be? *The Wind in the Willows* lies prone on her bedside cabinet. One glance is all it takes to convince Claudia that she does not imagine it, for the god Pan no longer sits on the front cover. Both badger and mole remain, their spellbound expressions suggesting they have fallen for his charm as deeply as she has. She remembers. Then…

I know what you have done.

Hadn't the god Pan spoken those words?

Yes, but he had also said she could right the wrong.

Still he does not turn to face her, nor is she brave enough to approach him. Instead, she leans her back against the door, the cool of the wood filtering through her clothing, and listens as the music turns more somber. The red hairs on his back stiffen, and his pointy ears twitch as the tune from his pipes takes on a physical form and floats toward her. She reaches up and captures a handful of fragrant air, feeling its density, its warmth, in the palm of her hand.

It's the sound of forgiveness, captured in waveform.

The music mellows, grows soft until it fades to nothing—as does he. Claudia holds the last scrap of warmth in her hand, reluctant to let it go.

If the great god Pan can forgive her, then she must find it in her heart to forgive herself.

STACEY

COFFEE AND COOKIES in hand, Stacey peeks in at the library, hoping to find it empty. Her hands shake too much to carry the damn cup up two flights of stairs, and she has no intention of sitting in the dining room with the old man.

A passing rain cloud darkens the room, erasing all shadows. She sniffs the air. The room smells like an old school. The kind of school where posh kids go. All polished wood and overcooked cabbage. She sits in what she now considers *her* chair and dunks the first Hobnob in the coffee before devouring the soggy mess whole.

The devilish heart she drew on the board has disappeared. Squinting in the dimness, she reads the message that has replaced it:

> *Please, whoever reads this, I beg of you, phone the police. And an ambulance, too. It might not be too late to save him. My husband's name is Kevin Richards, and I think I may have killed him.*

I am sorry, but I cannot give you any further information.

Fuck! She was right. The woman killed her husband. Stacey wonders what he did to deserve it. She knew he was the one to blame. Fat chance that someone calls for help, though. This frigging house is run by ghosts.

In the time it has taken her to read the words on the board, she has finished bar one of the Hobnobs. She licks melted chocolate from her fingers, then dunks the last remaining cookie in the cup. Half of it breaks off. It dawdles on top of the coffee for a brief moment, taunting her before sinking to the bottom. Shit! She dives in with thumb and forefinger, but it's too late. The half cookie melds with what is left of the drink, turning it into a mush. She pushes the cup away, annoyed by its deception.

So, the old man's dog is dead, and the woman has murdered her husband. What's next? It suddenly dawns on her. Tomorrow it will be her turn. She swallows hard, the part-digested cookies threatening to come back up. The urge to escape rears its head again, making her feel trapped. If she hadn't got on the stupid bus in the first place this would never have happened. Why did she? Where had the bus come from? And what had she been doing beforehand? Stacey rifles through the junk inside her head, but the answer is nowhere to be found. No doubt it will appear in the morning. Right here in this room. This place of accusation and judgment. It should be called a courtroom, not a library. She casts her gaze around the room, drinking in shelf after shelf of books, then dismisses it with a snort. She won't come. Simple as that. They can try as hard as they want, but she'll not be stepping one foot in here tomorrow morning.

ON REACHING THE first-floor landing, she thinks she hears music. Weird shit, like from a kid's film or something. She misses her music so much! There's fuck-all to do here except read.

Chapter Three: The Shadow Before

Mike, one of the characters in the novel, phones six long-lost friends from Derry, telling them they must come home. Something about fulfilling a promise and facing their demons. None of them know why they must return, and yet they feel compelled to do so. There is the suggestion that whatever they are about to face is terrifying beyond imagination, and yet they heed the call. Most of them, anyway. While five make arrangements to travel, one of them commits suicide by slashing his wrists in the bathtub rather than face the past.

Stacey puts down the book and draws breath deep into her lungs, holding it there as long as possible. The similarities between what is happening to her and what is happening in the story keep stacking up. It's as if Stephen King knows her.

A gurgling sound comes from the bathroom. The cobra stirs, tightens its grip on her arm. She stiffens and tunes in to the sound of water swirling down the plughole. Then another sound, barely a whisper, but familiar.

"Stacey… Help me. I'm dying."

Stacey leaps to her feet, covers the expanse of the room in four paces, and throws open the bathroom door.

Nothing.

No one.

The sink is bone-dry.

HOWARD

HOWARD FINDS HIMSELF alone in the dining room at lunchtime. *Strange,* he thinks. It's as if whoever runs the place knew he would be dining alone. No place setting has been laid for either Claudia or Stacey.

He removes the silver cloche, pleased to find a lamb chop and all the trimmings, then sprinkles a little pepper on the cabbage before tucking in.

On his left, a fresh fruit trifle, and on his right, a small plate of cheese and biscuits. He rubs his tummy. The flesh above his elastic waistband has filled out these past few days. He slides two fingers a little higher, surprised to discover he can no longer feel his ribcage through the fabric.

As he tucks in to the trifle, he thinks about Claudia and whether or not she has come to terms with the message on the blackboard. If so, she will have erased it. Perhaps he'll take a peek in the library before returning to his room. He hopes she has, because then she will feel better, like he does.

THE DOOR TO the library stands closed, denying him entry. Howard pauses, listens, then knocks on the door with one knuckle. Nothing. He knocks again, with his fist this time, but is met with silence. Howard takes hold of the handle and turns, but the door is firmly locked. He is a little disappointed to discover this, because he had hoped to find something to read. Now that he is feeling more settled, the time he spends in his room is beginning to drag.

His legs struggle with the stairs after such a heavy lunch, but his room offers a cheerful welcome. Sunlight pours in through the window, the morning showers chased away by its brilliance. There, on the dresser, is a white paper bag, folded at the top. He opens it and peers at the contents. Peppermints. Round white peppermints. He sniffs, then takes one out and licks the edge before putting it in his mouth.

"They're not for you." The voice startles him. He drops the bag and turns around, surprised to see Stacey standing in the doorway. "They're for the horse," she says, sniffing.

"You put them there?" A trickle of saliva escapes as he speaks, and he wipes it with his finger.

"No."

"Then who? H-how?"

She drags her nose along the sleeve of her sweatshirt. "Dunno, but they're not for you." A dismissive shrug, then, "Just saying."

Howard approaches the window, and is surprised to see the horse's head jutting from the stable door. He opens the window and takes a deep breath. The stamp of a hoof, the nod of a head. The horse is impatient to see him. The relief of not having imagined it is immense. Howard senses Stacey's presence at his shoulder. "Do you want to see him? Up close, I mean?"

Her face is a sheet of parchment that has not yet been written on. She pauses before answering. "Dunno."

She skulks behind him down the stairs, out the front door, and across the courtyard to the stable, hands shoved deep in pockets and head down. He hears her hesitancy in the drag of her feet on the gravel, and yet he knows she would not be following him if she wasn't curious. Stacey is not the kind of person to do something she doesn't want to.

The horse snorts as they get close, eyes wild. It nods its head in greeting.

"Good boy," Howard says, his voice smooth as chocolate spread.

Stacey stops a few feet from the horse, her attention on the sole of her boot as it draws an arc in the gravel.

Howard slips the paper packet from his pocket and palms one of the mints. "Here, boy. This is what you want, isn't it?" The horse flares its nostrils and whinnies, the whites of its eyes bright.

"Peppermint," she says.

"Yes, horses like peppermints. Like all good things, though, they should be consumed in moderation."

She sniffs. "His name, I mean."

"I beg your pardon?"

"Peppermint." She points at the horse. "It's his name."

Howard is taken aback. Who told her this? Is she making it up? His eyes search the stable door in case the horse's name is engraved there, but it isn't. The horse whinnies and stamps his hoof, eager for another treat. "Your turn," he says, holding the bag out to Stacey.

She shakes her head and steps back. "I'll watch. You do it." "Nervous?"

Another sniff, then, "Maybe. I ain't never fed one."

Howard grins. "Well, you know what they say—no time like the present. Come on, I'll show you."

Her hand trembles as he flattens her palm. "Don't bend your fingers. That way he won't accidentally take a nibble." He places the peppermint on her hand. "Go on then."

The horse is keen, none too gentle, and Stacey flinches.

"Steady now. He won't bite. He's far more interested in the mint than your hand."

A flick of the tongue, and the mint disappears. Stacey grins and punches the air. "Woo-hoo!" She twirls on the gravel, sending a scatter of stones skyward.

Howard steals a scrap of her joy and keeps it for himself.

THEY TRUDGE BACK indoors, side by side. Her boots are louder than his slippers, the imprint they leave behind more marked, despite her waif-like appearance.

"He'll remember you next time," Howard says. "Horses are good at remembering people."

She nods. "He remembered you. How long has it been since you last saw him?"

Howard laughs. "Just this morning, when you watched from the window."

"No. I mean how long before that?" She sniffs the palm of her hand, where a trail of horse saliva remains, and wrinkles her nose.

Howard shakes his head. "We only met this morning. I didn't know they kept a horse here until then."

Stacey stops in her tracks, head tilted sideways and eyes narrowed. "But your daughter, Evelyn." She chews her lip, watches his expression change from pleasure to confusion. "She named him Peppermint because of the white mark on his forehead."

Howard's heart sinks like a stone.

CLAUDIA

CONVINCED THAT THE god Pan has given her permission to forgive herself, or at least to accept what she has done and move on, Claudia makes her way to the library. But now that she's here, she's not so sure. Part of her still hopes someone has seen her message about informing the authorities and acted on it.

The words written in baby-pink chalk look so innocent. How can they speak of such violence? *Because the chalk is not responsible, Claudia. YOU ARE.* Her breath is a shudder as she picks up the cloth. Squeezing her eyes shut tight, she swipes at the board as though swatting a fly.

She opens one eye to a cloud of dust motes floating in her vision, pale-pink and shaped like a swaddled baby. It hangs in the air before rocking gently toward her feet and disappearing. She squints in the direction of the board and sees that the random swipe of her arm has failed to remove the message in its entirety.

The words *blood, bastard,* and a faint trace of his name, *Kevin Richards,* remain, as well as a few smudged letters. Claudia sits at her desk and considers the stubborn words. She tries to calm her mind so that she can analyze precisely what she knows about them and how they relate to one another, but her head is full of flying insects. They buzz in her brain and flit from lobe to lobe, interfering with her electrical impulses so badly she worries she is having a seizure.

She cannot stand the noise, the incessant zap of electricity, so she gets to her feet, takes the cloth in hand, and wipes away every last trace of pink from the board.

A soft bloom washes over her from head to toe. A white dove in the gloom. She slumps to her knees and cries tears of joy. No more images of bloodstained T-shirts to torment her, no grinning melons or red-handled screwdrivers.

A flutter at the window demands her attention. There, on the lawn, is the god Pan. Half-naked, his goat legs jig to the tune of his pipes as he weaves a path between the flower beds toward the apple tree. She thrusts open the window, eager to hear the call of his tune one last time.

His shadow follows him, an elongated, blackened thing, and it dances just as joyfully as he does. She watches until he disappears from view. Only the faintest whisper of the flute now. Or is it the wind in the trees?

BACK IN HER room, and having eaten nothing since her meager breakfast, she prepares for dinner by brushing her hair and pinching her cheeks in an attempt to appear like a living person rather than a corpse. Her fingers trace the neck of the sweatshirt and the skin beneath the cuffs as though reading Braille. No trace of bruising remains. It has faded alongside her memory of the event.

IN THE DINING room, Howard is seated at the table, white cotton napkin open on his lap as he prepares to tuck into what looks like a steak and kidney pie. He smiles when he sees her, and she returns the gesture.

Claudia takes her seat at the opposite end of the table and lifts the domed lid, pleased to find that whoever has prepared dinner is aware of her delicate tummy. No steak and kidney pie for her. Instead, a colorful salad with haloumi and grilled peaches awaits.

"How are you feeling, Claudia? Better, I hope."

She glances at him. Salt and pepper eyebrows, one raised with concern, and a genuine twinkle in his eyes.

"Yes, Howard, thank you. A bit exhausted, but doing well."

The door opens and in bursts Stacey, all jerky shoulders and gangly hips that dance to whatever tune plays in her head. "Freaking starving!" she says, dragging out a chair.

Claudia and Howard exchange a look of quiet amusement before resuming their meal.

Stacey swirls strands of spaghetti round her fork and slurps. She glances left to right, her mouth full. "What?" she says, grinning. "You try and eat this stuff without making a noise. Freaking impossible!" She sprinkles a tablespoonful of Parmesan cheese on top of the remaining spaghetti, then points her fork in Howard's direction. "You know how to ride?" Flecks of tomato sauce speckle her chin, contrasting with her dark hair and pale complexion to give her a vampiric look.

Howard swallows hard. "Ride?"

Claudia sees the struggle in his Adam's apple and wonders what this is about. She puts down her cutlery and waits.

"Yeah, you know…the horse."

He shifts his gaze to Claudia before answering. "I think I know how, or at least I did once upon a time." He chews his lip, uncertain.

"Excuse me, have I missed something?" Claudia asks.

Stacey shrugs, then points again at Howard. "There's a horse in the yard. It's his."

Howard blinks in quick succession, his face reddening. "It's not mine. Don't be silly."

Stacey laughs. "Huh, you can't fool me." She turns to Claudia. "It's called Peppermint, and he showed me how to feed it."

Claudia's mouth falls open, and she gasps. "Howard?"

"No, no. She's got it wrong!" His face crumples, and his hands flap like a toddler. It's the most distressed she has seen him since the incident with the dog.

Stacey twists another forkful of spaghetti, then takes a long and exaggerated slurp.

"It's his. I ain't lying. Well, actually, it's his daughter Evelyn's."

He's sweating now. Beads of perspiration falter above his brow before trickling down his temples to join those on his upper lip.

The loosened knot in Claudia's stomach tightens its grip. "Stacey, don't be cruel."

Stacey leans back on the chair so that the two front legs leave the floor. "I ain't! And don't ask me how I know. I just do." She rolls up the sleeves of her sweatshirt, ready to do battle, and the chair legs hit the floor like a hammer. "Just because he can't remember, don't mean I'm lying."

Howard's eyes have turned to glass. He no longer focuses on either of them, nor on the steak and kidney pie. He is lost in the past.

The ensuing silence is discomforting. It makes Claudia's feet shuffle beneath the table. "Howard?"

He glances at her, jolted back to the present.

Claudia wonders if both of them have gone mad. Surely there's no horse here. She would have heard or seen it by now. Horses need exercise. The girl is hallucinating, she thinks. That's what this is, another of Stacey's withdrawal symptoms.

Stacey pushes back her chair and stands. Her expression is innocent enough, though a little peeved. "Whatever," she says, before stomping from the room.

The air is thick with questions, dark and brooding as the clouds that scud past the twilit window.

Howard sits, head in hands. "I don't know, Claudia. It's all so confusing."

"You think the horse is real?"

He nods. "It's real, and I think it recognizes me, too."

Claudia ponders his words. "And your daughter? Is Stacey right about that?"

Claudia thinks he might cry. His chin quivers as he speaks. "I told you, I don't know. The name, Evelyn, it sounds familiar, but I don't know."

Claudia thinks for a moment. "Do you think it's possible Stacey and your daughter know one another?"

"I doubt it. If I have a daughter, and I say *if* because I am not certain, she would be around the same age as you, not Stacey. You wrote about my dog Gus, but you didn't know him, did you?"

She shakes her head and swallows. "No."

Shadows flicker on the candlelit sideboard, whispering words of comfort to one another. Outside, a tawny owl hoots a message of foreboding.

"I am convinced we are here for a reason, Claudia. I just don't know what the reason is yet."

She chooses a dark red apple from the bowl in the center of the table and polishes it to a shine on her sweatshirt before replacing it.

"The words in the library, Howard."

He raises his head and studies her.

"As soon as I erased them, I felt better, like someone had wrapped me in a woolen blanket and fed me nectar from a gilt medicine spoon."

"That's exactly how I felt. And another thing, I feel more aware, less withdrawn—if you know what I mean."

"I do."

"We address each other by our names now, too. Have you noticed?"

She frowns. "Can't say I have."

He wags a finger. "Think about it. *We* do, but Stacey doesn't, not yet. Before our epiphany, neither of us was really conscious of the other. Our names were written on the jars of chalks, but we didn't use them." He pauses to let his words sink in. "I thought of you as *the woman* and Stacey as *the girl*, as though you were of little consequence."

The cogs of her mind whir. He's right, of course, though she hasn't considered it until now. "But I stayed at her bedside all night, making sure she was safe. You know, the night she was ill. If I didn't care, then why would I bother?"

His fingers drum on the table. "Instinct, perhaps? Who knows?"

"Maybe."

"Tomorrow," he says. "Do you think it will be Stacey's turn?"

"I guess so. If she turns up, that is. I wouldn't be surprised if she knows what's coming and stays in bed."

He rubs his chin and yawns. "We carried her before, and we'll carry her again if necessary, though I imagine she'll fight us every step of the way." He studies her from beneath heavy brows. "We need this, Claudia. Each and every one of us needs to be here. I feel it in these old bones."

She picks up the same apple and holds it in her fist. "I guess you're right. I'll see you in the morning, ready to do battle."

STACEY

WHY THE OLD man got so uptight over the horse incident is anyone's guess. It's nuts that he denies the horse is his. Either he's forgotten or he's lying. She doesn't know which. Ah well, it's his problem.

Belly full of pasta, Stacey curls up on the bed and tries to focus on the novel. It's strange, because the next few chapters are all about the characters trying to remember the past and what's brought them to where they are today. Kind of like what's happening here. The bullying scenes are ace, though. They get her heart pumping faster than swallowing a dexie.

Then there's the house on Neibolt Street, an abandoned old house, with a nose-less hobo who offers Eddie a blowjob in return for a dime. Scary as fuck, but it makes her laugh, too. The old man looked like a hobo when they first arrived, and this house on Lacelean Street is abandoned—kind of—apart from the three of them. She imagines the old man asking her for a blowjob and retches. Gross! He's cleaned up now, ever since the thing on the blackboard, but still no way would she do it. Not even for a grand.

The thing on the blackboard… It'll be her turn tomorrow. She dog-ears the page of the book and flings it aside. The cobra stirs beneath her sleeve, its muscular ribs flex and straighten as it slithers along her upper arm, slick with sweat. She issues a sharp tap to its head, freezing as she senses its fangs prod the skin. *Go ahead, baby*, she thinks. *Do your worst.* She doesn't say it out loud, in case it takes her at her word. She's not ready to die.

The strip light in the bathroom buzzes as she pulls the cord, then flickers before giving in to its inevitable purpose. She pees, brushes her teeth, then peels off the joggers and sweatshirt, and stares at her reflection in the mirror. Gaunt. Hollowed cheekbones and sunken eyes. Jesus Christ, even the old man would probably pass. She grins, and the cobra hisses in agreement.

ALL NIGHT LONG, she tosses and turns. One minute soaked in sweat, the next freezing cold. Get it over with, she tells herself. You know you can't avoid it. Whatever he writes on the blackboard, you'll have to face and live with the consequences. All bravado.

The next minute, she is determined wild horses won't drag her to the library. Uh-oh, no freaking way!

One thing she knows for sure, it'll be the old man who will write the message. Not the woman. The woman wrote the message about the old man's dog (whatever its name was, can't remember), then *she* wrote the message about the woman stabbing the man with the screwdriver. So there's only the old man left. He's bound to write something about her. Simple as that. Perhaps he'll make something up out of spite. Maybe it won't even be true. Why worry in that case?

Perhaps after all three of them have *learned their lesson*, the nutter who runs this place will open the gates, and she'll finally be free.

But free to go where? The life she led before coming here is a blurred photograph., monochrome and burnt at the borders, with very little detail in the center. It wasn't a good life, she knows. She can sense the negative vibes in every pore, every cell of her mind and body.

SOME TIME LATER, dawn pokes its nose through the crack in the curtains, rousing her from a dream-filled sleep. She's not sorry, because in her dream a bald-headed clown with tufts of red hair followed her around the garden. She sensed his presence rather than saw him, and only caught a glimpse here and there. A game of hide and seek. One minute, she believed she'd outwitted him. The next, he was there again, peeping from behind the apple tree, or crouched low behind a rosebush, ready to pounce.

There was a horse in the stable. A horse named Pennywise. If she could make it as far as the stable, she could mount the horse and ride hell for leather. But as she opened the stable door, the clown was already there, waiting. Only now, he wasn't a clown at all. He was the old man in a clown suit.

She rubs her eyes and flexes her leg muscles. Cramp in the back of the calf has been a bummer lately. "It's Peppermint, you stupid fucker," she mumbles. "The horse's name is Peppermint, not Pennywise. That's the clown's name." Cursing under her breath, she swings her legs out of the bed and stands on one leg. She stares at the crack of light while kneading her sore calf muscle.

The clock on the bedside cabinet reads half eight. She's missed breakfast, which doesn't matter, as she's never been able to eat first thing in the morning. She has half an hour to decide whether or not to meet the others in the library for what she's certain will be her turn.

She can't do it. She's had enough already, what with having to go cold turkey in this fucking hellhole. She'll get dressed as quick as she can and do a runner. Hide in the grounds. The other two won't catch her, she's too fast. The ache at the back of her calf suggests otherwise.

Into the bathroom to pee. She won't bother to wash or clean her teeth. What's the point? If she's quick and sneaky, she can slip out of the house before they realize she's missing. She thinks back to the day of her arrival. Because she arrived late, the library was locked, which means she'll only have to stay outdoors for an hour or so, then it'll be too late. She fist pumps the air in celebration of her cunning.

As she steps out of the bathroom, an item on the bedside table catches her eye. It wasn't there before, and she didn't even close the door, so how the hell did someone put it there without her noticing? She tiptoes across the carpet like a thief. The mystery object is actually three: a glass of water and two pills. She sniffs the glass, then dips in a finger. Definitely water. The pills are uncoated and yellow. She picks them up and cups them in the flat of her palm before turning them over. A central line down the middle, the top half is scored with the letter *C*, the bottom with the letters *DB*. Valium. Five milligram, too. She shoves both pills in her mouth at the same time and swallows. Christ, she could have done with these days ago! At last, someone is sitting up and taking notice.

Are they, though? How freaking convenient that the pills have arrived half an hour before she's supposed to be in the library. Did the woman put them there? Nah, she'd have heard her, and in any case, if the woman was able to get her hands on some scoobies, she'd have given them to her the night she was sick, surely. Whoever runs this place has put them there, for certain. They want her in that library and are doing everything they can to make sure she goes. The rebellious side of her feels more determined than ever to stay away, but deep down she knows running only means delaying the inevitable. *Time to face your demon*, she tells herself before downing the rest of the water to encourage the drug to hit the spot sooner rather than later.

HALFWAY DOWN THE second flight of stairs, she meets the other two on their way up. The woman, who is in front, stops dead.

"We… We thought—"

Stacey hitches a shoulder toward her ear and continues down the stairs at such a pace she overtakes them both. "Let's get this show on the road," she says, rubbing her hands together, her words more confident than her heart.

The door handle is ice cold, more snow cone than brass. She flinches at its nip as she turns it and enters.

The blackboard's face is a blank stare. It gives nothing away. She swallows hard and scrapes the wooden chair across the floor before slumping down with feigned indifference for what she knows will happen soon.

The old man and the woman take their seats in a more decorous manner, the man clearing his throat and the woman fidgeting with the lid of the jar of chalks in front of her as though uncertain whether to open it or not. Stacey wonders what would happen if either of them took a second chalk instead of her. Would they know what to write this time? Or would they pass it to someone else like before? She'll wait then. Brazen it out and see if either of them acts first.

Under her breath she sings the words to Eminem's *Lose Yourself*, upping the volume and drumming a rhythm on the desk with the flats of her hands as she reaches the chorus, which makes the old man swivel to stare at her. It's bullshit, though, and she knows it.

Nothing happens for several minutes as each of them waits for Stacey to take the bait. Eventually, the woman turns to face her. "Well?" she says, her voice catching. She gives a little cough. "You ready?" She wears an encouraging smile, but beneath the curl of her lips, Stacey sees she is nervous. This woman knows Stacey is as unpredictable as a bull shark, that's why.

Stacey takes a deep breath, then untwists the lid and dips in her hand. Yellow. The brightest color in the jar. Such a cheerful color will be incapable of condemning her, won't it? Her hand trembles, but she tells herself it's the Valium rather than the nerves that's causing it. Her mind is as empty as the board. Left to her own devices, not a word would be written.

The old man knows what to write, though. She knew it would be him. He holds out his hand, flat palm and furrowed brow. The hand of Jesus, she thinks, which feels odd, as she's a non-believer. And the image of Jesus on the cross is accompanied by the scent of summer roses.

In the last few moments, her head seems to have developed a twitch. It jerks sideways, repeatedly, as though pulled by an invisible string. The old man's hand is cold against her warm one, unlike his expression, which is one of regret. He rises to his feet, all stiff, then shuffles toward the blackboard.

A wave of panic rises in her as he begins to write. A tsunami that threatens to sweep her off the chair and wash her away with the tide. She closes her eyes and wills the wave to come. It doesn't, and when she opens them again, she sees the words he has written with an unsteady hand that makes them difficult to read.

Lisa is dead.

He's still writing, but those three words are the seismic wave she's been waiting for. She leaps to her feet in an effort to escape the flood, knocking over both desk and chair in her haste. Eyes fixed on the door, it is all she sees. A yell of desperation, frustration, as the door handle fails to turn no matter how hard she rattles it. The fuckers have locked her in!

Terminator vision scans the room, searching for an escape route. The woman remains in her seat, mouth agape. The man continues to scribble on the board, oblivious to the fact that her world has come crashing down. She does not read what else he has written. There is only one way out of here—the spiral staircase that leads to the tower.

The cobra hisses a warning. It knows the tower is forbidden, as does Stacey. It says so in the file, but right now, she would prefer to risk the wrath of whoever is up there (if indeed there is anyone) than remain in this claustrophobic torture chamber.

"Stop!" the woman yells as Stacey flies up the first few stairs. Neither Stacey nor the man pay any heed. He continues to write, an automaton in motion, and she continues to race up the stairs as though chased by a demon.

She's almost at the top when the stench hits. An acrid reek that burns her throat and makes her heave. It doesn't stop her though, nothing will stop her. The relief of making it to the top turns to terror when she sees the bed. It stands at the center of the room, all crumpled sheets and stained pillows.

And then there's the girl.

The sight of her sister sprawled on her side turns her legs to jelly. A slip of a thing, rigid and blue, all angles.

On hands and knees, Stacey crawls toward the bed. "Lisa?"

A tumble of dark curls around Lisa's face. Her favorite Nirvana T-shirt, from which a nickel chain peeps. Stacey reaches forward and tugs at the chain, revealing a skull charm. Red-gemmed eyes, a black-toothed grin. How the fuck? Stacey is certain it's the necklace she was wearing when she arrived.

She shakes her sister by the shoulder. "Lisa! Wake up!" The skull chain rattles, red eyes glint, but the girl does not wake.

Beneath the letters *I* and the second *N* of the T-shirt are two small breasts, pierced nipples with stainless steel hoops, and inside that flesh, trapped in a cage of bones, rests a fist-sized heart that no longer beats.

Arms thrust skyward, she rests her weight on her haunches and emits a guttural howl of despair. Despite the noise, the girl in the bed does not move a muscle.

Lisa is dead.

Skin mottled purple, a dried crust at the corner of blue lips.

Stacey meets her sister's vacant gaze. Her own pupils are black holes, dying stars that feel the pull of gravity toward the person she loves most in the world, loves so acutely that in this moment she would swap places with her without hesitation.

In contrast, Lisa's pupils are pinpricks, no longer capable of allowing a single candela of light to enter.

A pool of vomit stains the bed sheet, a darker stain at hip level. Stacey grips the sheet tight in her fists, searches her sister's face in the vain hope that some fragment of life remains. All hope is dashed when she sees that Kurt Cobain's famous doodle of a baby swimming after a dollar bill has, by some trick of sorcery, transformed. The baby no longer chases the note. Instead, it lies on the bottom of the pool, drowned. The slogan, *COME AS YOU ARE*, blurs through uninvited tears. Beyond crying, her heart is a stone. A hardened gray lump that pumps poison instead of blood.

HOWARD

UNTIL HE PLACES the last full stop, Claudia's cry for help falls on deaf ears. Howard turns to see her standing at the foot of the spiral staircase. One hand clenches the rail, the knuckles bone-white. The other hand points skyward. It takes several seconds before her face comes into focus. Until then, it is a warped image, all snarling teeth and googly eyes. A froth of words that make no sense spew forth from the hole that is her mouth. It crosses his mind that perhaps he is having a stroke, but soon the fog clears, and his brain awakens to her shrill alarming call.

A glance over his shoulder confirms that Stacey is missing. As Claudia speaks, it becomes clear that she has climbed to the upper story without having been given permission to do so.

From up above comes a pathetic wailing sound, like a wild animal caught in a trap, or the cry of a banshee, warning of death. The air is tainted with the tang of decay, subtle but distinct.

"Help me, Howard!"

Claudia's command startles him back to the present. He places the bright-yellow chalk on the shelf and staggers toward her, a little off balance. "She's up *there*?"

Claudia nods violently. "Foolish girl!" She glances at the blackboard and blinks successively, as though the message thereon is too abhorrent to read. "I guess it has something to do with that." She gestures toward the words, shielding her eyes with a hand.

"Stacey?" His voice carries up the spiral stairs, an echo of concern. "Come down now. You shouldn't be up there."

Stacey pays him no heed. Instead, she continues to moan while Howard considers what to do next. He begins to climb, vaguely aware of Claudia's tentative footsteps behind him. Up, they spiral, her breath a cold breeze on the back of his neck.

Two steps from the top, he stops. The scene in front of him is so shocking, it is hard to take in. Stacey kneels beside a bed, upon which a young girl lies dead. Stacey's left hand clutches the stained sheet while her right hand strokes the pale cheek of the deceased. The wail has morphed into a whimper.

"Stacey?" Howard's voice is a soothing whisper, fearful it might break the spell and turn her into the savage beast she was moments earlier. She continues to ignore him, or perhaps she is oblivious. "You might want to stay where you are," he says to Claudia, turning to face her. "It's not nice up here."

Claudia's breaths are shallow, her face white as a sheet, but she shakes her head. "If she can bear it, then so can I."

He climbs the last two steps, then sidesteps to allow Claudia access. Still, Stacey does not move. Other than the bed in the middle of the room, the space looks much like the one below, lined with bookshelves and other paraphernalia. Behind the bed, an arched window is set into the wall, criss-crossed with diamond panes of glass. A ray of sunshine breaks free of the cloud and snoops inside, its beam falling on the dead girl's face and turning her alabaster complexion to moon dust.

The warmth and light effect a change in Stacey. "She's warm," she utters. For the first time, she glances in their direction, beckons them forward. "I think she's alive."

Claudia surprises Howard by striding toward the bed. She kneels and gently removes Stacey's hand from the dead girl's cheek before placing two fingers on the girl's neck and lowering an ear to her mouth.

Stacey screws her eyes, balls her fists, and moans.

Claudia takes her by the shoulders. "She's dead, Stacey. She's been dead for some time."

Stacey elbows out of her grasp, shaking her head. "Her face... It's warm."

Claudia shakes her head. "It's the sun. The sun has warmed her skin, nothing more."

Stacey trembles uncontrollably. Her teeth chatter, her speech is a stammer. "S-she can't be d-dead!"

And then Howard sees it. Beneath the sleeve of Stacey's sweatshirt, something writhes. At first, she seems oblivious to the movement, but then with a cry of pain, she whisks the garment off and throws it on the floor, revealing skeletal ribs and small breasts, flattened further by a black crop top. Howard flinches at her state of undress.

On the floor, the head of a cobra protrudes from the cuff of the sweatshirt. It tastes the air with its forked tongue, then out it slithers, eyes watchful. The hiss is a dog-like growl, a sharp warning.

Both Howard and Claudia freeze. The snake holds them captive as it weaves a path across the floor and up onto the bed in the direction of the dead girl. A glance at Stacey's upper arm reveals a tattooed rose, complete with thorns and two spots of blood. Face white as a sheet, Stacey watches the serpent's progress, paralyzed with fear.

The serpent wends its way along the dead girl's thigh, causing nothing but the soiled sheet to stir, before continuing up the torso toward her face. It pauses beneath the chin, tasting the rank air with an even fouler tongue, then stands tall, as though under the spell of a charmer. Hood spread, it turns to face them.

"*T-O-X-X-X-I-C!*"

The word it spits is delivered with a grin, the *X* in the middle elongated, like a hissing cat. A stream of venom flies through the air. A warning as opposed to a strike, as the poisonous fluid lands on the bed, not them. Its hooded head displays two circles—false eyes—and its skin glistens as though wet. A jaw opens wide enough to swallow a small mammal whole.

It strikes the dead girl's face. But its intention is not to devour her. Instead, it thrusts its head between her bluing lips and slides inside.

"No!" Stacey launches forward, fingers clawed and elbows at ninety degrees.

Claudia grabs one arm, Howard the other, and together they tussle Stacey to the ground. She kicks and writhes, spewing a barrage of profanity before falling still.

Claudia kneels on the ground, holds Stacey close and strokes her damp hair, shushing her like an infant.

When Howard senses her relax, he releases his grip and kneels in front of the bed, breathless and spent. The dead girl's torso ripples. The dead baby on the front of her T-shirt punches and kicks, then all is still.

The sun hides its face behind a dark and brooding cloud, shocked by what it has witnessed. The room dims. In the far corner, in the darkest part of the room, a candle flickers before it is extinguished by some invisible hand.

And the stench of death is replaced by the scent of the Damask Rose, powdery sweet. Howard closes his eyes and breathes in the heady scent, grateful for a moment's respite.

When at last he opens them, the bed has disappeared, taking the dead girl and the serpent with it. All that remains is an old library, a broken girl, a woman who is past her prime, and a man who is far too old and tired to deal with such trauma.

STACEY

THE MESSAGE ON the blackboard is a yellow blur, the warmth and strength of the two people she has come to know over the past four days the only reason she can bear to look at it.

The woman named Claudia helps Stacey back into the sweatshirt in an attempt to quell her shivers, then wraps a protective arm around her shoulders, whispering words of comfort that refuse to serve their purpose. Numb. Anesthetized in readiness for the post mortem that is still to come.

The old man, Howard, apologizes profusely for having written the message. Gray pallor, pinched lips. "I don't know what came over me," he says. "I—I never intended..."

Stacey shakes her head. It isn't his fault. She's been in his position and knows the power the chalk has over them. He pulls out a seat for her, before slumping into his own. He cannot look at the board. His guilt is too acute, too raw. It has not yet had time to fade.

Claudia pulls up a chair and sits next to Stacey, stroking her back as if she were a cat. The feral feline will not turn its claws on her, not now. Its temper has been tamed by what it has witnessed. She sees Stacey struggle to read the words. "Shall I read it to you, or would you prefer to leave it till later?"

Stacey knows she must face the inevitable. Each of them has had their turn, and until she accepts what has been written, she cannot erase it. The demon will rule eternal, and besides, after what has occurred, she knows what it will say.

She dabs at her eyes with the sleeve of her sweatshirt, then squints again in the direction of the board.

> *Lisa is dead. The cocaine you procured caused high levels of toxicity which resulted in arrhythmia and eventual cardiac arrest.*
>
> *On discovering her corpse, you fled, taking what remained of the drug with you.*

Claudia examines the fingernails on her left hand, flicking each in turn with her thumb because she does not want to witness Stacey's pain.

Howard tugs at his bottom lip, shaking his head from side to side with small movements. He cannot look at her, because the guilt cuts like a knife.

A shuddering sigh escapes Stacey's lips. She turns toward him. "What does the word beginning with *A* mean?

He lifts his head and looks her in the eye. His own ache behind the sockets, hers are threaded with bloody capillaries like miniature red rivers. "Arrhythmia?"

On his tongue, the word sounds musical, though she doubts its meaning is sweet. She nods and waits as he takes a deep breath.

"An abnormality of the heart's rhythm." It is not Howard that answers, but Claudia.

Stacey turns to face her.

"The drug will have caused a change in the sodium and potassium ion channels in the heart, thus affecting its electrical system." Having spoken the words, she shakes her head and blinks, as if she does not know where in the brain the information stemmed from.

A dense silence falls on the room, even the dust motes poise mid-air.

"I see," Stacey says, pulling at a thread on the cuff of the sweatshirt and unraveling it. She winds it round and round her finger, a coiled gray thing that threatens to cut off the blood supply. "I killed my own sister then."

Neither Howard nor Claudia contradict her.

Expression solemn as the grave, Howard gets to his feet and heads toward the door. "I'm sorry," he says. "I need some air."

Stacey and Claudia watch him leave, unsurprised when the door opens without complaint. It hadn't intended to let *her* out, that was all. Not until the lesson had been delivered. She feels no anger toward whoever locked it, no self-pity. The sister she loved with all her heart is dead, and she is to blame. No one else.

Sliding out of Claudia's half-embrace, she stands and approaches the board. Before wiping the words away, she shakes the cloth, freeing the last particles of what were once Claudia's condemnation into the air. A pale-pink pardon. Total absolution.

Cloth in hand, she pauses before wiping away her sister's name. The pain of doing so is a punch to the gut, but once the name is erased, the rest of the words fall like soldiers on the battlefield until no trace remains. Again, she shakes the cloth, this time making a plume of yellow particles dance. Each is a speck of sunshine, a tiny ray of hope.

"I'm going for a walk. I need time to think," she says, her voice hoarse and raspy.

"Would you like company?" Claudia's offer is genuine, but Stacey shakes her head.

"No. I need to be alone."

AS SHE PASSES the rosebush, she notes the smell of decay. The last few blooms are wilting. She continues to walk until she is as far away from the house as possible. She tucks up small, in a corner dark with shadow. The earth beneath her feet is soft. It crumbles to the touch. Time and time again, she picks up a handful, crumbles it to dust, and lets it fall.

Lisa. Her sister's face is a double image—one alive, the other dead. Try as she might, she cannot recall the life they shared, and yet the love is deep. It sits between her left kidney and pancreas, issuing sharp kicks to her spleen until she cries out in pain. She cannot recall when she gave her sister the drugs, but there is no doubt in her mind that she did. One of the few possessions she arrived with was a half-bag of coke, which she snorted the same night. The same baggie she had stolen from her sister. Why did it not kill her? It wanted her to live with the guilt, that's why. It would be easier to die and never know the misery and suffering she caused. She owns it, wholly, though she wonders why she ran away instead of calling for help.

The pocket of love issues another sharp kick, this time extending all the way to the bowel. It has a voice. A young voice, sore from smoke and slurred with alcohol. It is

Lisa's voice. *Because you panicked*, it says. *And because back then, the half a bag of coke was more powerful than your love for me. And besides, you knew it was too late. Nothing would have saved me.*

SOME TIME LATER, she gets to her feet, her spine sore from squatting.

The house is in darkness, apart from one room on the first floor, which she is certain is Claudia's.

About to enter the front door, the sound of a horse whinnying makes her turn toward the rear courtyard. Howard is there, and Peppermint too. No longer stabled, Howard leads him by the bridle. Shoulder to shoulder, they circle the yard, the horse's hooves a calming *clip-clop* on the cobbles.

He sees her and waves, but she is not ready for small talk, so she lowers her head and turns away.

"Stacey!" he calls. "Come and say hello. He's very gentle."

She shakes her head, but Howard and the horse continue to approach. It is the first time she has seen Howard smile, or at least she thinks it is. His breath mingles with the horse's to form a cloud. A fog in the garden of gloom.

The flank of the horse is warm. It thaws a sliver of ice in her heart and turns it into a smile.

"Come," he says. "Give him a peppermint." He holds out his hand, revealing a round white sweet that makes her stomach curdle. The horse nods its head, eager to devour the treat.

Before she can refuse, Howard passes her the sweet. "Remember what I told you. Tuck in your thumb and keep the hand flat."

Its tongue is probing, warm and dry. The mint disappears before she has a chance to think. The horse snorts, and she starts.

"He's saying thank you," Howard says, using his elbow to gently push the horse away. "He knows I have more in my pocket and has no concept of moderation. Tell you what," he points in the direction of the ménage, "how about I teach you to ride? We'll start tomorrow, if you're feeling better."

Head down, she shrugs. "I doubt it."

The horse nods. Its eyes are dark pools that reflect her despair. It senses her pain, she's certain.

Howard points toward her room on the second floor. "I'll bring you something to eat later. I don't imagine you'll be up to coming to the dining room."

The thought of food makes her gag.

"You must eat," he says, and his face is an open book. "Lisa would want you to."

Choking back the tears, she turns away and enters the house without looking back. As she hurries up the stairs, she makes a solemn promise: when she gets out of here—if she gets out of here—she will stay clean. This much, she owes to Lisa.

CLAUDIA

CLAUDIA REPLACES THE copy of *The Wind in the Willows* on the library shelf and scans the bookcase with little enthusiasm. It's no use. Convinced *The Wind in the Willows* had been put there for her, nothing else is of interest. And besides, her mind is elsewhere, trapped between worrying about Stacey and what tomorrow's lesson might involve. Now that they've all had their turn—their wake-up call—she cannot imagine what will happen next.

She wanders over to the window and drinks in the view. Hardly a leaf remains on the red maple, and the sweet chestnut is laden with spiky green fruits which should see the squirrels through the winter. As if conjured by her thoughts, a gray squirrel darts along a branch and turns to face her. *I see you*, it seems to say as it gnaws on whatever it holds in its paws.

This house on Lacelean Street has held her captive for the last four days, not only in the physical sense, but emotionally too. It has cosseted her in warm quilts and clean clothes. Served her favorite foods at regular intervals. Provided a place for convalescence. And yet, at the same time, it has come close to destroying her.

Claudia thinks about her companions, Stacey and Howard. The house has done the same for them, the same *to* them. A benevolent god? Or a troublesome demon? Is the house itself responsible? Or does a housekeeper lurk behind closed doors, watching their every move? If so, she's seen neither hide nor hair of them.

Until now, she hasn't considered how long they might stay or what might happen if and when they are set free. Since she cannot remember her past life, other than in vague flashbacks, she does not know whether she wants to return to it or not. Will she be arrested for murder? This place offers safety and solace from the outside world.

A sound startles her. She turns her gaze away from the window and back into the room. On a small round table is a taxidermied fox and cat. Neither of them made the sound. The fox remains seated on hind legs, front limbs crossed and a book resting on its lap. It studies the cat through wire-rimmed spectacles, a cat that bows low before it like a servant to its master. In its left paw, it carries a note.

Claudia stands before it and stoops to read the brass plaque on its case. *Sir Tibert delivering the king's message*, it says, and now that she's read it, the title makes sense.

But what made the sound?

She listens, half-hoping it will come again, and it does. It comes from up above, the second floor of the library. A scratching sound, like a mouse rearranging its den. It sends a shiver up her spine, resuscitates the abhorrent memory of what occurred up there earlier. It seems like a lifetime ago, the dead girl in the bed and the snake. A cobra, she thinks, though she's not clued up when it comes to identifying animals. The cobra that had once been part of Stacey's tattoo had come to life and—

She can't bear to think about what happened next. Poor girl! What an awful thing to witness.

NOT A SOUND comes from Stacey's room. Claudia pauses at the door, afraid to knock in case she is asleep. Instead, she turns the handle and peeps inside. Stacey lies on the bed in a fetal position, dressed only in underwear, her hands pillowing her face. She looks so young, so vulnerable, that it would not surprise Claudia if she caught her sucking her thumb.

Two dried pinpricks of blood sit next to the rose tattoo on her triceps, and something else, something Claudia is certain was not there before. She has bathed this girl, toweled her dry, and helped her to dress on more than one occasion, so she knows that the word *Lisa* was not there previously. She would have asked about it if it had been, perhaps as a topic of conversation. She tiptoes two steps closer. She is not mistaken. The tattooed word, *Lisa*, is fresh, the skin around it reddened.

On the bedside cabinet is a plate containing three chocolate biscuits and a sliver of fruit cake. One of the biscuits has a bite mark. A cold cup of coffee stands next to it, a protective skin on the surface. Howard must have brought it for her, she assumes. Both she and Howard have warmed to Stacey the last few days, even more so after what happened this morning. In outlook, they are worlds apart and would never have spent time with each other under normal circumstances, but these are not normal circumstances. Far from it.

She watches the rise and fall of Stacey's ribs for a few more seconds, then tiptoes from the room.

THE FOLLOWING MORNING, Claudia and Howard are the only guests to appear at breakfast. Nothing unusual there.

"I'll go and check on her soon, take her a glass of juice and a slice of toast," Claudia says.

Howard picks at a smoked kipper, his appetite nothing like it had been a few days earlier. "I took her a snack yesterday, but I doubt she ate it."

Claudia puts down her spoon and folds her arms. "I wonder what they have in store for us today?" She nods in the direction of the library.

"God knows, but I doubt it will be cause for celebration."

TO CLAUDIA'S SURPRISE, Stacey is up and dressed. She has showered, too. Damp hair sticks close to her head, giving her an elven appearance.

"You okay?" Claudia asks as she places the toast and juice on the bedside cabinet.

"Suppose. Ain't got much choice." She drains the juice but refuses the toast. "Wanna know something?" Her eyes twinkle, a fierce light in the dark. "I'm done. When I get out of here, I ain't never touching another drug in my life."

Claudia smiles. "Good for you. Lisa would be proud." How many times has she uttered these words? With a different name, perhaps, but the phrase feels familiar on her tongue.

Stacey pulls on her boots and bends to tie the laces. "I'll do it for her, otherwise she died for nothing." Her words are a seeping wound, and Claudia has to look away.

THE LIBRARY IS waiting for them. Claudia feels its breath against her cheek as they enter, hears the creak of its wooden bones as they approach their desks. This morning, the room smells of beeswax and blossom. Any trace of death and decay has disappeared.

The blackboard stands tall, a new message, written in blue chalk on its face.

> *You are permitted to climb the stairs. On the first floor, in a section of the library marked 'Biography,' you will find what you are looking for.*
>
> *Warning: Handle with care!*

"I ain't going back up there." Stacey gets to her feet and heads toward the door. She was last to enter and knows for a fact that she didn't close it behind her. Not after yesterday's fiasco.

"Come and sit down, Stacey. It'll be all right," Claudia says.

Howard stands and approaches the spiral stairs. One hand on the rail, he turns to face them. "I'll go first, and if there's anything untoward, I'll let you know. All right?"

Claudia winks at Stacey. "Don't fret. I'm sure it'll be fine."

Stacey's face is ghostly white, her eyes dark and sunken. The hair on the top section of her head has spiked as it dried, making her appear more pixie than elf.

Howard's voice floats toward them, a hollow echo. "There's nothing here, nothing but books anyway."

Claudia stands and holds out a hand. "Come on, you'll be fine."

"I can't!" Stacey sits with her head in her hands. "It's too raw."

Claudia places a hand on her shoulder. "You can do it, Stacey. The worst is over. Now all that's left is a pile of old books. Come on, we'll go together."

The climb to the top seems to take forever, but Howard stands above them, offering words of encouragement as they climb.

They step into a circular room, seeing it afresh, now without any hint of death.

"See?" Claudia says. "Nothing but books." Her heart races, but she is glad nothing more sinister lies within these walls. Already the events of the previous day feel like a dream. A nightmare.

Today is a new day, a better day. A day upon which they will take the next step toward enlightenment.

HOWARD

BOOKCASES ARE LABELED from left to right in alphabetical order. Howard has been keen to explore this floor of the library since his arrival, as his reading preference is for non-fiction. Unlike Stacey, however, he would never have disobeyed the rules.

Archaeology, Art... He traces the shelf with his finger until he reaches *Biography.*

While Claudia and Stacey cast their gaze around the room, he begins the search.

"Look," Claudia says, pointing toward the ceiling. "I didn't notice that yesterday." All three tilt their heads skyward. High above is a domed ceiling, upon which a celestial sky has been painted. More planetarium than library, the starscape is breathtaking. An ethereal nebula in the night sky.

"Woah." Stacey stands, hands on hips, and gawps. "It's kinda like heaven."

Howard points. "The Orion Nebula. One of the closest and most active stellar nurseries in the Milky Way. Look, there's his belt."

"It's moving." Claudia shakes her head in disbelief.

She's right, a cloud of dust and gas swirls before their eyes, changing color as it travels—muted reds and heathered blues, all of which emit a faint phosphorescent glow.

Howard sees the glint in Stacey's eyes and knows she is fighting back tears. "Wasn't Orion some kind of hunter?" she says, and the muscles in her throat tense and relax as she swallows.

"Indeed." He draws an outline in the air. "There's his shield, and there's his sword. Do you see?"

"Are those his hunting dogs?" Claudia says, following a trail of stars with her index finger.

"Canis Major and Canis Minor, though they're far more visible here than they would be to the naked eye."

As they speak, the swirling mist above their heads continues to roll, taking on a three-dimensional aspect, so much so that Claudia has to wave a hand in front of her face to clear it. The mist dissipates, and the air is sharp and bright with miniature specks of crystal, like one's first step outside after fallen snow.

Howard sways on his heels, his balance off-kilter. "Did you know, Orion was blinded as punishment for his sins? Eventually, his vision was restored by Helios, the Titan god of the sun and sight."

Claudia frowns. "Strange," she says. "You can remember all this and yet you can't remember your own past."

Howard's face falls, saddens. "You're right, and the same can be said of all of us." He wrings his hands. "Hopefully the biographies will enlighten us, though I may need some help in locating mine since I don't have my glasses."

Stacey wanders over to the large reading table that now stands in the middle of the room, where yesterday a bed stood—a bed upon which her dead sister lay. She picks up a magnifying glass and hands it to him. "Here, this might help."

Returning to the bookshelf marked *Biography*, Howard begins to browse. "Strange," he says, beckoning the women over. "The spines are unmarked."

The bookcase on which the biographies are located consists of eight shelves, each of which is filled with identical volumes, bound in tawny leather. The only difference being that some are thicker than others. He plucks one from the shelf at random and weighs it in the palm of his hand. A blank cover. No title or author's name, and certainly no illustration. He opens it and flicks through from front to back. The paper is the old kind—creamy white and thick—but not a word is printed inside. "More like sketchbooks," he says, puzzled.

Stacey walks her fingers along the second shelf and pulls out another. "Here, this one has a name on the spine. Claudia Dance," she says, passing it to Claudia. "I guess it's yours."

Claudia flushes as she takes it from her.

"Cool name, by the way," Stacey says, grinning. "Claudia Dance! Who'd have guessed?"

The volume in Claudia's hand is substantial. She balances it on her flattened palm, testing its weight, before scurrying off with it, like a dog with a bone. Her property—no one else's.

Stacey blows her fringe out of her eyes and follows it up with a series of jerky movements that resemble a stringed puppet.

Howard beams, his face bright red. He holds the magnifying glass to his eye and studies her, his left eye hugely disproportionate.

"Freak!" She jumps back in an exaggerated manner. "You remind me of Mike from *Monsters, Inc.*"

"What's your surname?" Howard asks, lowering the magnifier.

She pauses for a moment, scratches her head, then claps and points. "Alloway!"

"Then I guess yours will be on the top shelf."

Before he has a chance to look, she elbows past him and stands on tiptoe. "Aha! Got it!" The volume is slender, no thicker than her ring finger. She wanders off without offering to help Howard locate his.

With the help of the magnifier, it doesn't take him long, though his knees protest as he lowers himself to the floor. Bottom shelf, *Howard Wilson*. The volume is by far the thickest of the three, the spine a little worn, a little faded, as if it has been read on many occasions. Howard's heart races. He wobbles as he gets to his feet.

He tucks the magnifier in the elastic waistband of his joggers, then raises the volume in the air, his arm straining with the weight. *Mine's thicker because I'm old*, he thinks, acknowledging the burden of decades in his spine, as well as in his hand. "I'm taking it downstairs," he says. "See you later."

The sound of slippered feet on wrought-iron stairs goes unnoticed. Neither woman so much as raises her head.

THE DINING ROOM will be far more comfortable than his bedroom for reading. Facing south, and with large bay windows, it will be brighter too.

The smell of freshly brewed coffee embraces him as he enters. A blazing fire in the hearth ensures he stays. He places the volume on a pedestal table, next to a comfortable armchair, and wanders over to the sideboard. Two cubes of brown sugar and a dash of cream, the coffee looks and smells delicious. He selects a pastry and returns with the refreshments.

The book rests on the table, giving him the eye. He tries to ignore it, wishing to delay the inevitable. He sips the coffee, devours the pastry, then returns to the sideboard for another, before finally picking up the book. Resting it on his lap, and with the help of the magnifier, he begins to read.

Written chronologically, the opening chapters hold him spellbound. Each name he reads, each place he visits, springs to life before his eyes, the memories of his past rising from the pages.

He reads of his daughter, Evelyn, and is able to picture her face. Stacey had been right, then. How strange. But she wasn't the only one with clairvoyant perception. It had happened to him, too. Somehow he had known Stacey's sister's name. Not only that, but he had also known the cause of her death.

Evelyn… The light of his life. The daughter once granted the gift of a horse for her fourteenth birthday. A horse named Peppermint. Replacing the book on the table, he steeples his fingers and considers the possibility of that horse and the horse in the stables here being one and the same. If true, then Peppermint would be more than forty years old now. Impossible! And yet, he's certain it's the same horse.

It is the final few chapters that threaten to undo him. They remind Howard of how he became a recluse. Wealthy, yes, but oh so lonely.

Howard puts down the book and pinches the bridge of his nose in an attempt to stem the tears. Who is he crying for? Himself, or those he has lost?

And of course there is Gus, his death the final straw. The memory of Gus, his one true companion, opens the floodgates.

The biography ends with Gus's death. The last sentence reads: *As the last spade of earth hit the ground, Howard turned away from the house and wandered into a night black as pitch, leaving all his worldly possessions and memories behind.*

Howard takes a deep, stuttering breath. The last section of the book contains blank pages, thirty or so at a guess. They are to be filled with the last years of his life, if indeed he has years left to live. His eighty-first birthday is on the horizon. Time is not on his side. The clock above the mantle ticks an ever-constant rhythm, a reminder of time's eternal existence. Whether Howard is in the world or not, time will continue.

He places the book on the table and considers what to do next.

The fire in the hearth spits. Nothing but dying embers. If Howard wishes to remain in this room, he will need to add fuel to the flames and breathe new life into them.

STACEY

ONE CHAPTER IN, and Stacey can't breathe. Invisible hands wrap around her throat, threatening to cut off her airway. Without so much as a word to Claudia, she leaps to her feet and runs down the spiral stairs with the speed of a gazelle.

She doesn't care that it's raining. In fact, she doesn't even notice. Her one thought is that she is desperate for air.

As tempting as it is to tear every page from the book and scatter it to the wind, she knows she dare not, so she heads for the farthest corner of the garden, squats down beside the wilted blooms of the rosebush, and continues to read.

A mother addicted to alcohol—a woman she fails to picture because she had no contact with her from the age of three. A young life lived through the hands of the care system, *care* being a bone of contention, as it is clear that none of it was spent happily. Apart from the three years she and Lisa spent in the care of their grandmother, the rest were a swirling pit of sewage, a spiraling tornado of self destruction at the hands of those who were meant to keep them safe.

A life shared with kids like them, kids with too much baggage, from whom they learned that *to trust* was to open yourself up to abuse.

From the age of ten, she and Lisa, just two years younger, were fostered out time and time again, only to end up right back where they started. Unwanted. Unloved. A living hell.

Damp earth seeps through her joggers, and the book's pages darken and kink with the weight of the rain and her thoughts, but she does not seek shelter.

When her knees stiffen to the point of pain, she places a hand on the ground and adjusts her posture. A sharp prick to the palm, blood trickles along the life line and onto her wrist, before seeping into the cuff of her sweatshirt. A rose thorn, once buried in the earth and disturbed by the weight of her hand, is the culprit. It protrudes from her thumb pad like a vampire's tooth. She plucks it out, then wipes the blood on her sleeve and examines her life line. Short. And worse still, a broken start to the line. Perhaps this is why her book is slender. Claudia's book felt heavy, thicker than hers. She had assumed it was because she was younger than Claudia, but perhaps it means her entire life will be short.

A voice floats on the breeze—a whisper of a voice—but one she recognizes nonetheless. "Stay strong," it says. "You have it in you, girl." It is the voice of her grandmother. A wilted petal twirls from the bush to her outstretched palm. She crushes it in her fist and inhales a faint trace of her grandmother's scent.

Grief prevents her from reading the final chapter, and the blank pages that follow go unnoticed. The image of Lisa in the bed is too fresh. An open wound that continues to weep. She closes the book and heads indoors.

THE URGE FOR a fix is intense, the demon more powerful than it has been for days. A hundred sit-ups and twenty press-ups later, she feels no better. She downs a glass of water, her mind following the icy chill as it snakes around her organs, and shivers.

The only distraction in the room is Stephen King's *It*. She grabs the book and lies on her chest on the floor, crossing and uncrossing her legs behind her. If only she had her phone. Music might help.

After reading the same paragraph three times, it dawns on her that this particular chapter is all about Mike Hanlon's research into the past, an assembling of the history of Derry. As the town's librarian, he has access to past resources and uses them to compile a volume which he locks in the library's vault. As such, he is both seeker and keeper of its past history. Jesus fucking Christ. Yet another parallel between King's fantasy world and the one she's currently immersed in.

Derry's murder rate is six times the norm. Sounds like her town, shithole that it is. Except the only real clown is her. Stupid cow, messed up her life, and her sister's too. And for what? The anger is a fireball no hydrant can extinguish.

A tap at the window demands her attention. Seconds later, another tap. She gets to her feet and wanders over. Howard stands there, complete with a handful of gravel and a clown-like grin. Beside him is the horse, Peppermint.

"Thought you might fancy a riding lesson. It's stopped raining." Peppermint snorts and stamps his hoof.

She hesitates for a moment. *Ah, fuck it! Might as well.* She opens the window wide. "I'll be down in a minute." Stephen King's *It* is discarded on the rug without so much as a sweet wrapper to mark the page.

CLAUDIA

ON THE TOP floor of the library, Claudia takes up residence on the chaise lounge beneath the arched window and opens the volume to the first page.

The Life of Claudia Dance

Her heart skips a beat. How is it possible that a book has been written about her? As soon as she sees her parents' names, she remembers. Joan and William Dance. Their smiling faces loom large, though a worried frown lurks behind her father's gaze.

The first few chapters reveal her childhood, and everything comes flooding back. She had wanted to be a dancer, wanted to live up to the surname she was proud of, and despite the strain on the family's finances, her parents had sent her to ballet and ballroom lessons. A typical, happy childhood.

The air in the library chills—shifts—as though she has been transported to another room entirely. She pauses her reading and scans the room. She can't remember Howard and Stacey leaving, so she is surprised to find herself alone. The memory of the previous day's occurrence delivers a shred of doubt. What if the horrific tableau reappears and she finds herself alone with Stacey's dead sister? But of course, the scene was not intended for her. It was Stacey's disobedience of the rules that made it happen.

She raises her eyes skyward and sees that the shift in atmosphere has been caused by a shift in the sky. Not the real sky. The sky that has been painted on the ceiling. Oh, but it is so much more than a painting. It is, for all the world, as if the space above her head is infinite. She is certain that if she were able to climb a ladder to the top, she would touch only air, not plaster.

She puts down the biography and stands. The air is crisp and sharp, cloud-free. Above her is an entirely different constellation altogether. No huntsman and hounds. Instead, five stars shine bright in the shape of an arrowhead.

Astronomy or *Astrology*? She is uncertain which is which as she searches the shelves. There are several books on both subjects, but she selects one called *The Easy Guide to the Night Sky:Discovering the Constellations With Your Eyes and Binoculars* and returns to the chaise.

Although the guide is relatively simple, it takes her a while to discover that the constellation above her head is Capricornus. Claudia skims much of the text, eager to return to the story of her own life, but one particular passage demands her attention. Capricornus, it says, represents the Greek god Pan. For a moment she imagines she hears the sound of his pipes, but it is just the wind whistling down the chimney.

According to the reference book, Pan, in an effort to escape a monster, dived into a river and attempted to turn himself into a fish. However, things did not go according to plan and he was left with the head and body of a goat, and the rear section of a fish. The sight amused Zeus, and so he put the image into the stars as the constellation Capricornus.

Claudia thought the god Pan had finished with her, but now she is convinced he has come to watch over her while she unpacks the minute detail of her past life. Such a comforting thought.

According to the biography, things take a turn for the worse when Claudia reaches her teens. Her dream of becoming a dancer is soon quashed when she finds herself pregnant at the age of sixteen. The book relates the facts around the subsequent abortion in such a matter-of-fact manner that she has to pause and take stock. A baby girl. Bile rises to her throat. Did she have any other children afterwards? If so, she has no memory of them, not yet. She thinks back to the plume of pale-pink chalk dust in the room downstairs, a baby-shaped bundle that floated in the air before disappearing, and weeps.

The god Pan looks down from the celestial ceiling, determined to help her through the subsequent chapters. Chapters so harrowing she runs the whole gamut of emotions: terror, anger, devastation, grief, despair, even a sprinkle of happiness here and there.

Many chapters cause her to pause and take stock, to assimilate the knowledge she is fed and make sense of it. Why did she allow those things to happen? What a fool she has been!

A career in nursing, which makes sense when she considers her aptitude in dealing with Stacey's predicament. The words she had spoken to Stacey, *Lisa would be proud of you*. No wonder they had felt familiar on her tongue. The image of former patients spring to mind, those who faced trauma and fought hard. She had spoken those words on many occasions, knowing she lied, because in truth they meant little, especially if the person she referred to was already dead, as in Lisa's case.

It is reading about her marriage that is hardest to stomach. The years of abuse. Decades of mind control that eventually turn to physical violence. Capricornus's stars twinkle above her head, the god Pan promising light at the end of the tunnel no matter how dark things may seem. And there were no other children. According to the book, she and Kevin tried for a few years before she lied to him and decided to bitterly swallow the birth control pills rather than raise his child.

Kevin has stolen her life. She considers this for a minute or so before concluding that she is as much to blame for not having the courage to break free. But back then, she failed to muster the strength. It was never as simple as walking out. It never is.

Right now, she is grateful for the fact that she has no children. Yes, they would be adults now, but what a nightmare it would be for her to try to explain that she has murdered their father.

The final chapter, that which details the incident that caused her to flee that night, is gruesome enough in its detail to make it a certainty.

Which brings her right back to the present.

Claudia flicks through the blank pages at the end of the book, wondering what words will appear there in future. A life of imprisonment, perhaps.

Pan twinkles an eye as she gets to her feet, and the cloudless sky darkens a shade.

STACEY

STACEY'S INNER THIGHS and arse are sore as hell, but she can't remember when last she had this much fun. She thinks back to some of the craziest exploits outlined in her biography, the wicked days spent drinking and getting high. They seemed like fun at the time, and even now some of the things she got up to make her laugh, but they weren't fun. Not really. Not like learning to ride Peppermint. This is new, an exciting challenge, and what's more, it's all about trust. Coming here has been better than any rehab joint. Here, she has learned to trust, or at least she has started to. Who'd have thought? And among old folk, too! Well, Claudia's not *really* old, but Howard is. A lump forms in her throat when she thinks about them. They've helped her more than they know. They've been the parents she never had. How can she feel like this after spending less than a week in their company?

What would Lisa think if she saw her riding a horse? Well, maybe not *riding*, not yet. Not galloping, anyway. The gnawing ache returns when she thinks of Lisa and how she let her down. If she gets out of here, she will seek out her grave. A tidal wave of panic surges as she considers the possibility that no one has discovered the body yet. What if she's lying there, rotting? Jesus fucking Christ! She can't bear to think about it. She rushes to the bathroom and dry heaves over the toilet.

A tap at the door. Before she has a chance to answer, the door opens, and Claudia's there, a look of concern on her face. "You all right?"

Stacey sits with her back against the cold tiles, wiping a trail of spittle from the corner of her mouth. Glassy-eyed, she looks at Claudia and shakes her head. "I can't," she says. "I'll never be able to forgive myself."

An internal switch flicks to green, and Claudia's nursing skills light a beacon in the dark.

THE DINING ROOM is cozy and lamplit. All three are gathered together, like a family.

"Had to coax this one into coming down," Claudia says, nudging an elbow in Stacey's direction.

Howard winks at her. "You're going to need to fatten those bones a bit if you want to ride Peppermint. He'll think he's carrying a skeleton on his back otherwise."

Stacey nods and picks at the garlic bread, tearing off thin strips before eating them.

"I wonder what tomorrow will bring?" Claudia says. "I mean, what more can they tell us?"

Howard shakes his head. "Something tells me this will be our last supper."

The room falls silent, a parlor left vacant by mourners at a funeral.

"Perhaps they won't let us leave, like this is our punishment for the things we did," Stacey says.

"You think so? Would you be happy to stay?" Howard asks.

She bites her lip. "Dunno. It's kinda peaceful, and if we leave, I'll really miss Peppermint." She grins and waves a fork at both him and Claudia. "But it's kinda boring, too."

ANOTHER SLEEPLESS NIGHT ensues, but the following morning, she's ready in the hall before the others. She can't let Howard and Claudia down. Not after all they've done for her.

The library door yawns wide, welcoming them inside. "Woah, get this!" Stacey crosses the threshold first. Instead of jars of chalks, on each desk is a suitcase made of old leather, their initials engraved on the front. "Didn't they do this during the war?" She picks hers up and points at the letters: S. A. "You know, when they sent the kids away from the cities?"

"Evacuees, you mean?" Howard traces his initials in the leather.

Before Stacey can answer, Claudia draws their attention to the blackboard. "Look."

Stacey replaces the suitcase on the desk and folds her arms. There on the blackboard is a message, written in white chalk.

You have been good students on the whole, and now you are free to leave. The bus will depart at five o'clock today. Don't be late.

P. S. Everything you require for your onward journey can be found in your suitcase.

"Well, fuck me!" Stacey makes no apology for her language, even though Howard flinches. "That's me, that is. That bit there." She points at the board. "The bit that says, *on the whole.* Hah!"

Claudia springs the two catches of the suitcase, eager to see inside.

Stacey's bravado dissipates into thin air. This feels too intense, too scary. "I'm taking mine to my room," she says, hoisting the suitcase and leaving Claudia and Howard to gawp.

A WAD OF cash inside a brown envelope, a set of keys, individually labeled, an ID card with her photograph on the front, a passbook to a bank account, the balance not stated.

Beneath the black leather wallet containing these items is a set of clothing: black jeggings, a T-shirt with the slogan, *Spread Sunshine, not Shade.* Cheesy as fuck, but it'll have to do. Several sets of underwear, pajamas, and toiletries are also included.

She changes into the new clothes before opening the wardrobe and removing her leather jacket. It has not been worn since the day she was ill. She holds it in front of her. The breast pocket, where she kept her stash, is scuffed from overuse. She holds it to her face and inhales. A trace of skunk remains, but it fails to hit the spot because there's another smell too. The scent of her sister.

She puts it on and zips it up to hide the cheesy T-shirt slogan. She's lost weight, so the jacket sags a little at the waist. Instinctively, she pats the inside pocket, the pocket where she kept her phone, surprised to find it there. She hesitates before pulling it out, because she knows that in the contacts folder, the names of all the people she knew in her past life lurk. She swallows hard, deeply aware that all she needs to do once she gets a signal is message any one of them, and her problems will start all over again. Unable to resist, she whips out the phone and switches it on. A flash of blue light, then a sigh of relief when she discovers the phone is brand new and blank.

Not a single name exists, not even a song.

WITH SEVERAL HOURS to kill before the bus arrives, she tries to relax. Half-hoping that Howard might call her to say goodbye to Peppermint, she remains on high alert, jumping at the slightest sound. He doesn't though, and she's not brave enough to go herself. Too chicken to say goodbye to the horse without Howard there, because she knows she'll get upset.

She picks up the novel and attempts to read, but her mind is a whir. Ah, fuck it! She doesn't want to find out what happens to the characters anyway. If her memory of the movie is anything to go by, the clown gets them in the end, and right now, that's not what she needs to read about. Too many similarities. She doesn't want to think about the fuck-faced clown that might be waiting for her when she gets out of here.

CLAUDIA

BY HALF FOUR, Claudia is ready. She has emptied and re-packed the contents of the suitcases no less than six times and still can't believe it. Her stomach is in knots. She has wished the last few hours away, but every minute has dragged. It's not that she's desperate to leave. In fact, she dreads it. Every possible scenario has resided in her head over the past few hours, and she cannot bear it much longer. She'll miss both Stacey and Howard. They have shared something so intimate over the last week that they feel closer than family. Each of them has bared their soul.

She waits five more minutes before picking up her suitcase and going downstairs. In the hallway, the grandfather clock marks time, its heartbeat the only sound. Claudia puts down the suitcase and sits on the same velvet chair she sat on when she first arrived. No card with her name on it now. The table is adorned with a vase of white lilies, nothing else.

If the other two don't show soon, she'll go and look for them. She cannot bear the waiting much longer.

At a quarter to five, Stacey appears, dragging her suit-case down the stairs. She looks exhausted, bone-weary. Events this week have taken their toll. Claudia watches her approach, and her stomach relaxes a fraction.

"You seen Howard?" Stacey asks, putting down her case and shaking the stiffness from her arm.

"No, not since we left the library. I couldn't face lunch."

"Me neither." She jerks her head several times and blinks rapidly. "Shall I give him a knock?"

"I guess so. The last thing we want is to be late."

Claudia drags the suitcases to the front door and waits while Stacey runs back upstairs.

Within a matter of seconds, she returns. "He's not there." Her face is ashen. "Where the hell can he be?"

Claudia glances at the clock: eleven minutes to the hour. Dusk has already fallen. If Howard is in the garden, it won't be easy to find him. "Shit," she says, wringing her hands. "You try the library, I'll check the dining room."

Moments later, Claudia calls. "Stacey? Come and see this!" The fire blazes bright, as though recently fed. Claudia points at the flames. "Do you think—"

A hungry flame licks at the cover of a book, its leathered face shriveled and black. Without hesitation, Stacey snatches it up and blows on the flame. "Fuck!" She waves it in the air, sending a whirl of cinders to the floor. A few lines are still legible, though charred and smoke-damaged.

"Look," Stacey says, "I'm sure that says Peppermint. We should have guessed. He's with the horse. Perhaps he's finding it hard to say goodbye." And with that, she tears from the room, leaving Claudia with no choice other than to wait.

Six minutes to five. Anxiety mounts in her chest until she thinks she might have a heart attack. In the last few minutes, the sky has dimmed at least two shades, and dark gray clouds have gathered to watch.

She picks up both suitcases and drags them into the courtyard. "Stacey! We must leave now, or we'll miss the bus!" The sound of her frantic call echoes around the yard, and despondency deepens. If they do not make it out today, they will not be given another chance. This she feels in her heart. If Stacey doesn't come soon, she'll leave without her. The thought of doing so makes her head spin. The walk to the bus stop, the wait, the journey to God-knows-where. She can't do it, not by herself.

The sound of running feet on gravel offers a ray of hope.

"He's not there," Stacey says, and Claudia sees her despair even in the dim light of an autumn evening.

"Then we must go without him. The bus will be here any minute." She picks up her suitcase and steps forward.

"No, you don't understand!"

Claudia turns to face her.

"Howard's not there, and neither is the horse. There's not even a whiff of Peppermint in the stable." Her eyes are pleading. Two dark pools of panic. "It's as if he never existed."

Claudia shakes her head. "Listen to me, Stacey. If we don't go now, it's over. Do you understand?" Her voice cracks. "And besides, Howard would want us to."

For several moments, she believes Stacey will stand defiant. Her fists are balled, her mouth twisted. Then, without another word, she picks up her suitcase and follows Claudia to the gate.

With her left hand, Claudia grasps the bolt. At first, it does not yield. But then, with an audible click, the bolt slides open.

A hundred or so yards to the bus stop, and yet it seems a mile away.

No time to consider the strangeness of the situation. No time to reflect on the fact that a week earlier, they arrived at this same spot in a catatonic state.

The wind whips about their faces, doing its best to drive them back, but they battle on. The sign on the opposite side of the street reads LACELEAN ST., though it's difficult to make out in the encroaching darkness.

Stacey spots it first. "Look," she says, pointing up the road. The appearance of the bus hastens them on.

It jerks to a halt, its bright-yellow paint the only color in a world of gray. LACELEAN ST., the electronic display on the front reads, and Claudia's stomach drops. Expecting the doors to whoosh open, she is surprised when nothing happens. The inside of the bus is dimly lit, though she is certain the driver's face looks familiar. Same stern expression, unreadable. She knocks on the door, eager to climb aboard, but instead of opening it, he fiddles with something on the dashboard, a digital display of some kind.

"What the fuck?" Stacey says, banging her fist against the glass. "Hey, you gonna let us on or what?"

He ignores them still, then points toward the windscreen and leans back in his seat.

A sound from the front of the bus, a digital clicking sound. Both Stacey and Claudia stare at the destination sign. In front of their eyes, the letters rearrange themselves, luminous yellow letters that a moment ago read LACELEAN ST. switch places.

"Oh my God!" Claudia says, grabbing Stacey by the elbow. "Look!"

In bright bold capitals, the destination sign now reads CLEAN SLATE.

With a whoosh, the doors open, and they climb on board. The driver pays them no attention. He starts the engine, and the bus pulls away from the curb with a judder.

Stacey follows Claudia down the aisle, stopping halfway. "Window?" Claudia says, and Stacey nods. They haul their cases onto the seat in front, and Stacey takes the window seat. They peer into the darkness as the bus travels along the road, in the opposite direction from which it arrived.

As they approach the house at the end of the street, Claudia hooks Stacey's arm in hers and senses no resistance.

In the encroaching twilight, it is just possible to make out the wrought-iron gates and the looming tower of the library.

Everything else is a gray ghost.

Stacey presses her forehead to the cold glass, her breath condensing. "Why, Howard? You should be here with us." On breath-misted glass, she traces his name.

Howard

Beneath it, she draws an upside-down mouth. A stray tear rolls down her cheek, and Claudia taps her own shoulder.

Stacey leans her head on Claudia and drifts. Dark, wet eyelashes on porcelain skin. So delicate, Claudia thinks. As fragile as a snowflake.

The bus rumbles onward. It is so dark, it is impossible to see where they are going. Claudia closes her eyes and tunes into the whir of wheels, the splash of puddles, the patter of raindrops against the window.

She dreams of the god Pan. He leads her by the hand toward a grassy hillock. Sunshine so bright it blinds her. His flute is a reedy breath of musical notes, and this time, she understands the meaning behind the tune.

Dance, Claudia…dance!

ACKNOWLEDGMENTS

A WRITER'S JOURNEY can be a lonely one, and yet there are many who help along the way.

First of all, I would like to thank my husband, Tony. You are my first reader, my harshest critic, my best friend, and my life.

Immense thanks and appreciation to Rob Carroll and the team at Dark Matter INK for believing in this story and providing the opportunity for it to reach others.

I must give a special mention to Tim McGregor for scrutinizing this novella in the early stages. Your enthusiasm and comments have helped make it a better book.

To my good friends in the Twitter community—you inspire me each and every day!

Last but not least, to each and every reader, my appreciation always. Without you, my work would have no purpose.

—Catherine McCarthy

ABOUT THE AUTHOR

CATHERINE MCCARTHY WEAVES dark tales on an ancient loom from her farmhouse in West Wales.

The House at the End of Lacelean Street is her most recent work of long fiction. Other work includes *Mosaic, A Moonlit Path of Madness,* and *The Wolf and the Favour.* Her short fiction has been published in various anthologies and magazines, including those by Black Spot Books, Nosetouch Press, Dark Matter Ink, and House of Gamut.

In 2020, she won the Aberystwyth University Prize for her short fiction.

Time away from the loom is spent hiking the Welsh coast path or huddled in an ancient graveyard reading Dylan Thomas or Poe.

Find her at catherine-mccarthy-author.com, or on Twitter/X @serialsemantic.

ABOUT THE ARTIST

TONY EVANS IS a photographer, illustrator, musician, and animator from Wales. After completing a degree in Fine Art, he spent his career as a lecturer, animator for a multi-media company, and managing the media support department of a university.

In 2017, at the Fusion North London International Film Festival, his music was officially selected as Best Original Music Score. In 2019, he had an honorary mention at the London Seasonal Short Film Festival and was also awarded the Armed Forces Community Covenant Award in 2019 for his animation.

His artwork has appeared in *West Wales Life&Style Magazine, The Four Faced Liar* literary journal, and on the front cover of *British Fantasy Horizons.*

He spends his free time slaving over book covers and creating animated trailers for his author wife, Catherine McCarthy, and relaxes by creating music, making movie props, and taking photographs of the West Wales landscape. See more at celtic-eye.com.

Also Available or Coming Soon from Dark Matter INK

Human Monsters: A Horror Anthology
Edited by Sadie Hartmann & Ashley Saywers
ISBN 978-1-958598-00-9

Zero Dark Thirty: The 30 Darkest Stories from Dark Matter Magazine, 2021–'22 Edited by Rob Carroll
ISBN 978-1-958598-16-0

Linghun by Ai Jiang
ISBN 978-1-958598-02-3

Monstrous Futures: A Sci-Fi Horror Anthology
Edited by Alex Woodroe
ISBN 978-1-958598-07-8

Our Love Will Devour Us by R. L. Meza
ISBN 978-1-958598-17-7

Haunted Reels: Stories from the Minds of Professional Filmmakers Curated by David Lawson
ISBN 978-1-958598-13-9

The Vein by Steph Nelson
ISBN 978-1-958598-15-3

Other Minds by Eliane Boey
ISBN 978-1-958598-19-1

Monster Lairs: A Dark Fantasy Horror Anthology
Edited by Anna Madden
ISBN 978-1-958598-08-5

Frost Bite by Angela Sylvaine
ISBN 978-1-958598-03-0

The Bleed by Stephen S. Schreffler
ISBN 978-1-958598-11-5

Free Burn by Drew Huff
ISBN 978-1-958598-26-9

The Dead Spot: Stories of Lost Girls
by Angela Sylvaine
ISBN 978-1-958598-27-6

When the Gods Are Away by Robert E. Harpold
ISBN 978-1-958598-47-4

Grim Root by Bonnie Jo Stufflebeam
ISBN 978-1-958598-36-8

Voracious by Belicia Rhea
ISBN 978-1-958598-25-2

Abducted by Patrick Barb
ISBN 978-1-958598-37-5

Darkly Through the Glass Place by Kirk Bueckert
ISBN 978-1-958598-48-1

Beautiful Ways We Break Each Other Open
by Angela Liu
ISBN 978-1-958598-60-3

Chopping Spree by Angela Sylvaine
ISBN 978-1-958598-31-3

The Off-Season: An Anthology of Coastal New Weird
Edited by Marissa van Uden
ISBN 978-1-958598-24-5

The Exodontists by Drew Huff
ISBN 978-1-958598-64-1

Saturday Fright at the Movies
by Amanda Cecelia Lang
ISBN 978-1-958598-75-7

The Threshing Floor by Steph Nelson
ISBN 978-1-958598-49-8

Club Contango by Eliane Boey
ISBN 978-1-958598-57-3

Psychopomp by Maria Dong
ISBN 978-1-958598-52-8

Little Red Flags: Stories of Cults, Cons, and Control
Edited by Noelle W. Ihli & Steph Nelson
ISBN 978-1-958598-54-2

The Divine Flesh by Drew Huff
ISBN 978-1-958598-59-7

Frost Bite 2 by Angela Sylvaine
ISBN 978-1-958598-55-9

Disgraced Return of the Kap's Needle
by Renan Bernardo
ISBN 978-1-958598-74-0

Dark Matter Presents: Fear City
ISBN 978-1-958598-90-0

Part of the Dark Hart Collection

Rootwork by Tracy Cross
ISBN 978-1-958598-01-6

Mosaic by Catherine McCarthy
ISBN 978-1-958598-06-1

Apparitions by Adam Pottle
ISBN 978-1-958598-18-4

I Can See Your Lies by Izzy Lee
ISBN 978-1-958598-28-3

A Gathering of Weapons by Tracy Cross
ISBN 978-1-958598-38-2

Printed in the USA
CPSIA information can be obtained
at www.ICGtesting.com
JSHW080542060424
60602JS00004B/226